Six Records of a Floating Life

Fu Sheng Liu Ji

Shen Fu

ISBN: 9798878184755
Imprint: Daybreak Studios

CONTENTS

Volume One: The Joy of the Bridal Chamber 1

Volume Two: Leisure and Pleasure 23

Volume Three: Troubles and Sorrows 36

Volume Four: Travels and Adventures 55

Volume Five: Zhongshan Chronicle 91

Volume Six: The Way to Health 128

PREFACE

"The Six Records of a Floating Life" is a shining pearl in the history of classical Chinese literature, renowned for its exquisite descriptions and profound character portrayals. The author, Shen Fu, with his unique perspective, condensed the minutiae of life into a refined literary work, leaving behind a precious cultural heritage for future generations.

In this work, we can not only feel the author's acute observation of life but also appreciate his delicate portrayal of the emotional world. Each story is like a delicate painting, vividly depicting the inner world of the characters. Whether it's emotional entanglements or the various facets of life, they are vividly expressed by the author's pen, deeply touching readers.

"The Six Records of a Floating Life" is not just a literary work but also a mirror of history, reflecting the social landscape and people's living conditions at the time. Through descriptions of officialdom, family, marriage, and other aspects, readers can not only appreciate the various situations of ancient society but also reflect on the relationship between human nature, society, and the individual in comparison to the present.

"The Six Records of a Floating Life" comprises six volumes, unfortunately, the final two volumes, "Zhongshan Chronicle" and "The Way to Health," have been lost to history. The versions of these two volumes included in this book are deemed to be forgeries based on expert studies. Nevertheless, they are included here for reference purposes.

Rereading "The Six Records of a Floating Life" today allows us not only to appreciate its literary value but also to draw wisdom from it, enlightening our minds and guiding us to ponder more deeply the meaning and value of life.

VOLUME ONE: THE JOY OF THE BRIDAL CHAMBER

I was born in the year of Guiwei of the Qianlong reign (1763), on the twenty-second day of the eleventh month of winter. It happened to be a time of peace and prosperity, and I was born into a scholarly family living by the side of Canglang Pavilion in Suzhou. The kindness bestowed upon me by the heavens could be said to be unparalleled.

As Su Dongpo's poem goes: "Events are like a spring dream, leaving no trace." If I do not record them in writing, it would be a waste of the heavens' benevolence towards me. Thinking of how the Book of Songs begins with the "Guoju" poem, I also decided to start with the affairs of a couple. The rest of the content will be written accordingly. What troubles me is that in my youth, I was not diligent in my studies, and my literacy was limited. I only recorded the true events of that time. If one must scrutinize the rhetoric and structure of the article, it is like blaming a mirror with stains for not being bright enough.

In my childhood, I was betrothed to the Jin family, but she passed away at the age of eight.

So I married into the Chen family. Chen's name was Yun, with the courtesy name Shuzhen, she was the daughter of my uncle, Mr. Xin. She was naturally intelligent and clever. When she learned to speak, I read her the long poem "Pipa Xing," and she quickly memorized it. Unfortunately, her father passed away when she was four years old, leaving only her mother and younger brother, Kechang, in poverty. As Yun grew up, she excelled in embroidery and weaving, and the three of them relied on her craftsmanship for a living. Even when Kechang went to school, there was never a shortage of money for his tuition.

One day, she found "Pipa Xing" in the book basket, and she recognized the characters word by word. During her spare time from embroidery, she gradually learned to write poetry, composing such beautiful lines as "Autumn invades, shadows thin; Frost dyes chrysanthemums plump."

When I was thirteen, I accompanied my mother back to her family. I got along well with her and had the opportunity to read her poems. Although I admired her elegant and beautiful thoughts, and worried about her short life, my heart was full of her, and I couldn't let go. So I said to my mother, "If I had to choose a wife, I would rather not marry anyone other than Sister Shuzhen." My mother also liked her gentle and meek nature, so she took off her gold ring and gave it to her, sealing the marriage contract. That day was the sixteenth day of the seventh month of the Qianlong year of Yiwu (1775).

That winter, her cousin got married, and I followed my mother to attend the wedding. Yun and I were the same age, but she was ten months older than me, so we still called her Sister Shu from childhood.

At that time, everyone in the room was dressed in bright new clothes, but Yun alone wore simple clothes, just changing into a new pair of shoes. I noticed that her shoes were exquisitely embroidered, and when I inquired, I found out that she had made them herself, realizing that her intelligence was not only reflected in her words. She had a graceful figure, with slender shoulders and a long neck, thin but not bony. Her eyebrows were beautiful, her eyes shining. Only her two teeth were slightly exposed, which seemed to mar her otherwise excellent appearance. But her charming and delicate demeanor made people irresistibly attracted to her.

I asked for her poetry manuscripts to read. Some were only a couplet, some only had three or four lines, most of them were fragments. When I asked her why, she smiled and said, "These are amateur works without a teacher's guidance. I hope to have a confidant who can be my mentor to help me refine them into complete pieces." I jokingly became her teacher and titled her poetry manuscripts with the words "Exquisite Phrases." Little did I know that the omen of Yun's short life was already hidden within.

Late at night, after seeing the relatives off outside the city, it was already past midnight when we returned. I was hungry, looking for food, and a servant brought dates, but I found them too sweet. Yun quietly tugged at my sleeve and led me to her boudoir, where I saw the hot porridge and side dishes she had prepared.

I eagerly picked up the chopsticks to eat, but suddenly her cousin, Yuheng, shouted from outside the door, "Shu, come out quickly!"

Yun hurriedly closed the door and said, "I'm already tired and ready to sleep." Yuheng pushed the door open and saw me about to eat the porridge. He smirked at Yun and said, "Just now I said I wanted porridge, and you said there was none left. Turns out you were hiding it here to specially treat your husband, huh?" Yun was embarrassed, hiding away, and the people in the courtyard burst into laughter. In a fit of pique, I pulled up the old servant and returned home first.

Since being ridiculed for eating porridge, whenever I went to Yun's house, she intentionally avoided seeing me. Of course, I understood that she was afraid of being laughed at.

On the twenty-second day of the first month of the Qianlong year of Gengzi (1780), on the night of the bridal chamber candlelight, I saw her slender and delicate figure, just as timid and shy as before. I lifted her veil, and we smiled at each other.

After the wedding, as we sat side by side, eating late-night snacks together, I quietly held her wrist under the table. Her fingers were delicate and warm, and my heart couldn't help but beat faster. It happened to be her fasting day when I offered her food; she had been fasting for many years. I secretly calculated that the day she started fasting was the day I had chickenpox. So I smiled and said to her, "Now that I'm unscathed, sister, can you stop fasting from today?" Yun smiled and nodded.

On the twenty-fourth day, it was my sister's wedding day, and the twenty-third day was a national mourning day, so we couldn't hold any celebrations. Therefore, we held a banquet for my sister's wedding on the twenty-second day. Yun accompanied the guests in the hall, while I drank with the bridesmaids in the bridal chamber, losing in every game of dice until I got drunk and fell asleep. When I woke up, Yun was already grooming herself.

That day, relatives and friends came in succession, and the festivities didn't start until the evening.

In the early hours of the twenty-fourth day, I, as the new brother-in-law, escorted the bride. I returned home at three in the morning. At that time, the lights were dim, and a maid was dozing by the bed, while Yun had removed her makeup but had not yet gone to bed, holding a candle and staring at a book with rapt attention.

I touched her shoulder and said, "Sister, you've been working hard these days. Why are you still so diligent?" Yun quickly turned around and stood up, saying, "I was just about to go to sleep, but I found this book when I opened the bookcase. Unknowingly, I forgot about tiredness while reading. I've heard about 'The Romance of the Western Chamber' for a long time, but only today did I get to see it. It truly lives up to the reputation of a talented scholar. It's just that the words between the lines are a bit sharp." I smiled and said, "It's because he's a talented scholar that his words can be so sharp." The maid urged her to go to bed and closed the door before leaving. Then I teased Yun, just like reuniting with a good friend. I reached into her arms, and her heart was pounding as well. I leaned in close to her ear and asked, "Why is sister's heart beating so fast?" Yun looked back at me, smiled, and felt as if a strand of affection was stirring our souls. I embraced her delicate body and entered the tent, oblivious to the fact that it was already dawn.

Yun was introverted and spoke very little when she first entered the door, but she never showed any unhappiness all day long. Even when talking to her, it was just a smile. She was respectful to her elders, gentle and kind to her servants, and organized in her actions, without any flaws. Every day when the sun rose, she would get up as if someone were urging her.

I teased her, saying, "It's not like the scene when we had porridge before, why are you still afraid of being laughed at?" Yun replied, "Back then, hiding porridge for you became a joke. Today, it's not about being afraid of being laughed at, but worried that my mother-in-law will say the new bride is lazy." Although I was reluctant to have her sleep away from my side, I also admired her actions, so I began to wake up early with her. From then on, we were close as if we were one, and the depth of our love for each other was beyond words.

However, happy times are easy to pass, and in the blink of an eye, it was already a month.

At that time, my father, Jiafu Gong, was serving as a prefect in Kuaiji and specifically sent someone to bring me to study under Mr. Zhao Xingzhai in Hangzhou. Mr. Zhao was a gentle and skillful teacher, and my ability to write today is all thanks to his teachings.

When I returned home to get married, it was agreed that I would continue my studies under Mr. Zhao afterwards. But when I received news from my father, I felt melancholy. I was worried that Yun would cry in public, but she forced a smile and encouraged me, even helping me pack my bags. That evening, I noticed that her expression was slightly different from usual.

Before parting, Yun whispered to me, "After leaving home, there's no one to take care of you. Be careful in everything." When I boarded the boat and untied the ropes, it was a bright spring day with peach and plum blossoms competing for beauty, but I felt as if I were a lost bird, and the colors of the world had changed. After arriving at the academy, my father crossed the river eastward.

I stayed at the academy for three months, but it felt like ten years away from Yun. Although Yun often wrote letters, they were mostly brief exchanges, mostly words of encouragement and pleasantries, which made me feel unhappy. Whenever the wind blew through the bamboo forest in the courtyard, and the moon shone on the banana trees outside the window, I would think of the past days spent with Yun, feeling as if I were in a dream. Mr. Zhao understood my thoughts and wrote to my father, explaining the situation, and set ten questions for me to temporarily return home. I was overjoyed, as if a soldier had been pardoned and returned home.

After boarding the ship, every moment felt as slow as a year. When I arrived home, I first went to my mother's residence to pay respects before entering my own room. Yun greeted me, and we held hands without saying a word, but our souls seemed to turn into smoke between us, feeling only a ringing in our ears, unable to feel where our bodies were.

It was June at the time, and it was hot and stuffy indoors. Fortunately, we lived in the west wing of the Ailian Residence by Canglang Pavilion.

Inside the plank bridge, there was a pavilion facing the water called "Wuqu," named after the phrase "Clear the tassel, muddy the feet." There was an old tree in front of the eaves, casting a dense shade over the windows, turning people's faces green, while tourists on the opposite side came and went.

This was where my father, Jiafu Gong, held private banquets.

After consulting my mother, I brought Yun here to escape the summer heat. Yun also stopped embroidering because of the hot weather, spending her days accompanying me in studying and discussing ancient texts, enjoying the moon and flowers. Yun was not good at drinking, but she could barely manage three cups. So I taught her drinking games from ancient times to liven up the atmosphere. I thought, perhaps, there was no greater joy in the world than this scene.

One day, Yun asked me, "Which school of ancient literature

should women learn from?"

I replied, "The 'Strategies of the Warring States' and the 'Zhuangzi,' for their agility and wit; Kuang Heng and Liu Xiang, for their elegance and vigor; Sima Qian and Ban Gu, for their vastness and breadth; Han Yu, for his richness; Liu Zongyuan, for his sharpness; Ouyang Xiu, for his elegance; the Three Sus, for their eloquence. As for others such as Jia Yi and Dong Zhongshu's debates, Yu Xin and Xu Ling's parallel prose, Lu Zhi's memorials and essays, there are too many places to learn from, all depending on one's own understanding."

Yun said, "The writings of ancient scholars are all about profound insights and grandeur. It may be difficult for women to enter. Only in writing poetry do I have some understanding."

I said, "In the Tang Dynasty imperial examinations, talents were discovered through poetry. And the masters of poetry must be Li Bai and Du Fu. Which one would you like to learn from?"

Yun discussed, "Du Fu's poetry is refined and pure, while Li Bai's is free-spirited and unconventional. If I had to choose between Du Fu's strictness and Li Bai's liveliness, I would prefer to learn from Li Bai's liveliness."

I said, "Du Gongbu is a master of poetry, and many people learn from him. Why do you choose Li Bai instead?"

Yun replied, "Du Fu's poems are strict and profound, and his words are mature and wise. Of course, this is Du Fu's specialty. But Li Bai's poetry is like a celestial nymph on Mount Miaogu, with a kind of elegance that flows like falling flowers and flowing water, which makes people feel admiration. It's not that Du Fu is inferior to Li Bai, but rather, I am more drawn to Li Bai's lighter and deeper thoughts."

I chuckled and said, "I didn't expect Chen Shuzhen to be a confidant of both Du Fu and Li Qinglian."

Yun smiled and replied, "I also have an enlightening teacher, Mr. Bai Letian. I often remember him in my heart and never forget his teachings."

I asked, "What does that mean?"

Yun replied, "Isn't he the one who wrote 'The Song of the Pipa'?"

I laughed, "It's really amazing! Li Taibai is your confidant, and Bai Letian is your mentor. I happen to have the character 'Bai' in my name, so I'm your husband. How coincidental that you have such a connection with the character 'Bai'!"

Yun smiled, "Having a connection with the character 'Bai,' I'm afraid there will be a lot of 'Bai' characters in the future." In Wu dialect, homophones are read as "Bai" characters.

The two of us laughed heartily without any prior arrangement.

I said, "Since you understand poetry so well, then you must also know how to distinguish the quality of prose, right?"

Yun said, "The 'Chu Ci' is the source of prose, but my knowledge is limited, and it's difficult for me to understand it deeply. If we're only talking about the Han and Jin dynasties, the style is ancient and the language is concise. It seems that Sima Xiangru is the best."

I joked, "When Zhuo Wenjun eloped with Sima Xiangru, perhaps it wasn't because of his qin skills, but because of his writing, huh?"

The two of us burst into laughter again.

I am straightforward by nature and not concerned with trivial matters, while Yun seems to be reserved and adheres to formalities.

Occasionally, when I helped her put on her clothes or adjust her sleeves, she would always say, "I'm sorry, I'm sorry." Sometimes when I handed her a handkerchief or a fan, she would always stand up to accept it. At first, I didn't like her behavior and said, "Are you trying to restrict me with etiquette? There's a saying: 'Excessive etiquette hides deception.'"

Yun's cheeks turned red, and she said, "Respect and courtesy are teachings. Why do you see them as deceitful?"

I replied, "Respect comes from the heart, not from these deceptive formalities."

Yun said, "The closest people are usually parents. Can you be disrespectful while holding them in your heart?"

I said, "I was just joking earlier."

Yun said, "Many conflicts in the world arise from jokes. Don't wrongly accuse me in the future, or it might make people feel suffocated to death."

I then hugged her and comforted her for a long time before she finally smiled. From then on, "I'm sorry" and "excuse me" became common phrases for us.

Like the ancient couple Liang Hong and Meng Guang, we respected and loved each other, living together for twenty-three years. The longer the time, the deeper our feelings grew. Whether inside the house or out on the small paths, whenever we met, we would hold hands and ask each other, "Where are you going?" We were cautious as if fearing the eyes of others. In fact, although we initially avoided others when walking together, over time, we stopped caring.

Sometimes when Yun was chatting with others and saw me approaching, she would stand up and move aside to make room for me to sit next to her. Neither of us ever thought about why we did this. At first, it felt a bit embarrassing, but afterward, it became natural.

I often wonder why some elderly couples treat each other like enemies. I wonder if there's any truth to the saying, "How can you grow old together if you don't have some quarrels?"

Is there any truth in this?

On the evening of Qixi, Yun prepared incense, candles, and fruits, and we worshiped the Weaver Girl together in the "Wo Qu Xuan."

I engraved a seal with the inscription "May we be husband and wife for generations to come," and Yun and I each held one with red and white characters for our correspondence. On the night of Qixi, the moon was exceptionally beautiful. Looking down at the river, the ripples were like silk ribbons. Yun held a light silk fan in her hand, and we sat side by side by the water, looking up at the ever-changing clouds in the sky.

Yun said, "The universe is so vast, and the moon is the same for everyone in the world. I wonder if there are others in the world tonight who are enjoying the moon like us?"

I said, "Enjoying the coolness and admiring the moon can be done anywhere. If we're talking about appreciating the beauty of clouds and mist, perhaps there are many people who, with a discerning heart, can appreciate them deeply in the secluded chambers of their homes. If it's about a couple admiring the moon together, they probably wouldn't be discussing clouds and mist, right?"

Before long, the candles burned out, and the moon disappeared behind the clouds. We cleared away the incense and fruits and went back to rest.

On the fifteenth day of the seventh month, the night of the full moon, commonly known as the "Ghost Festival," Yun prepared wine and food, intending to enjoy a drink under the moon.

That night, dark clouds suddenly covered the sky, and the atmosphere became gloomy. Yun furrowed her brows and said, "If I can grow old with you, the moon will come out." I also lost interest because of this. Only the fireflies on the opposite bank twinkled, weaving in and out between the willow trees and the docks covered in smartweed.

Yun and I played a game of writing couplets to pass the time and dispel our worries. However, after a few verses, the more we wrote, the more disorganized they became, and our thoughts wandered. Yun's eyes were already filled with tears and laughter, and she collapsed into my arms, unable to speak. I smelled the strong fragrance of jasmine on her temples, so I gently patted her back and used other words to ease the situation, saying, "It is said that in ancient times, jasmine was likened to pearls in shape and color, so it was used as a hair ornament. But little did we know that this flower must be tainted with the breath of oil and powder to emit its fragrance, making it even more intimate. Even the Buddha's hand used as an offering has to step back three steps."

Yun stopped laughing and said, "The Buddha's hand is a noble fragrance. Its scent is subtle and comes naturally, whereas jasmine is a lowly fragrance that needs human assistance, so its scent is like flattery."

I said, "Then why do you prefer the lowly fragrance over the noble one?" Yun replied, "I am jokingly preferring the lowly fragrance over the noble one."

As we were talking, it was already the middle of the night, and gradually, the clouds dispersed in the sky, and a bright moon emerged. Yun and I were suddenly overjoyed and leaned against the window to drink together. Before we could finish three cups, we suddenly heard a loud noise from below the bridge, as if someone had fallen into the water. Looking closely from the window, the water surface was as calm as a mirror, and we couldn't see anything, only hearing the sound of a duck rushing around on the riverbank. I knew that there were ghosts of drowning victims in the water near Canglang Pavilion, so I was worried that Yun would be frightened and didn't immediately explain.

Yun said, "Oh my! Where did that sound come from?"

It made us both feel a bit creepy. We quickly closed the window and went back to the room with the wine. At this moment, the room was dimly lit, with curtains hanging down, making it seem eerie and causing us to feel unsettled. After lighting the lamp and entering the tent, Yun had developed a fever. I also fell ill and felt dizzy and lethargic for about twenty days.

It's true what they say, "Too much joy brings disaster." This was probably a sign that we wouldn't grow old together.

During the Mid-Autumn Festival, not long after I recovered from illness, I thought about how Yun, my newlywed wife of half a year, had never been to the neighboring Canglang Pavilion. So, I instructed the old servants and gatekeepers not to let anyone else enter. As the evening approached, Yun, my younger sister, a middle-aged maid, and a young maid supported us. The old servants led the way, crossing the stone bridge and entering the eastern gate of Canglang Pavilion's garden. Inside the garden, there were stacked rocks forming hills, and lush greenery surrounded us. Canglang Pavilion stood atop a soil hill. We climbed the steps and entered the pavilion, where we could see smoke rising and a beautiful sunset several miles away. Across the river was "Near Mountain Forest," a place where the governor entertained guests. At that time, the Yishu Academy had not yet been built.

We laid out blankets in the pavilion, and we all sat on the ground while the gatekeeper brewed tea for us. After a while, the bright moon had risen above the treetops, and the cool breeze made us feel refreshed. Watching the moonlight shimmering on the water's surface, all worldly worries vanished in an instant. Yun said, "Today's garden outing is truly delightful! If only we could take a boat ride to and from Canglang Pavilion, wouldn't it be even more enjoyable?"

By now, it was time for the lanterns to be lit, and recalling the fright from the fifteenth night of the seventh month, we supported each other down the steps of the pavilion and left the garden.

In Wu dialect, there's a custom on the Mid-Autumn Festival night where women, regardless of their status, come out in groups to enjoy the moon, called "Walking under the Moon." Although Canglang Pavilion was elegant and secluded, surprisingly, no one else came.

My father, Jia Fugong, liked adopting sons, so I had twenty-six half-brothers from different families. My mother also had nine adopted daughters, among whom Wang Ergu, Yu Liugu, and Yun had the closest relationships. Wang Ergu was gentle and had a good alcohol tolerance, while Yu Liugu was straightforward and talkative. Whenever they gathered, they would chase me out to sleep in the outer room, and the three of them would share the same bed. This was Yu Liugu's idea.

I joked, "After my sister gets married, I'll definitely invite her husband to stay for ten days!" Yu Liugu said, "I'll come too! Sharing a bed with my sister-in-law would be even more wonderful, wouldn't it?" Yun and Wang Ergu smiled on the side. At that time, because my younger brother Qitang got married, Yun and I moved to Canglang Pavilion's Warehouse Rice Lane. Although the house was spacious, it lacked the tranquility and elegance of Canglang Pavilion.

On my mother's birthday, a theatrical troupe came to perform, which intrigued Yun. My father had no taboos and often had plays like "The Tragic Farewell" performed. The performances by the veteran actors were moving. While watching from behind the curtain, I suddenly noticed Yun leaving and not returning for a long time. I went to check on her, followed by Yu Liugu and Wang Ergu. We found Yun sitting alone at the dressing table, chin resting in her hand.

I asked, "Why do you look so distressed?" Yun said, "Watching a theatrical performance should bring joy. Today's performance only leaves one's heart in agony." Yu Liugu and Wang Ergu burst into laughter.

I said, "Yun is a sentimental person." Yu Liugu said, "Is my sister going to sit alone here all day?" Yun said, "Let's wait for a better play to come out."

Wang Ergu heard this and went out first to ask my mother to perform more enjoyable plays like "Stabbing Liang" and "Hou Suo." Then she persuaded Yun to come out and watch. Only then did Yun cheer up.

My uncle, Susun Gong, passed away early and had no descendants, so my father adopted me to be his son. His tomb was next to the Fushou Mountain ancestral tomb on the west side of West Crossing Pond. Every spring, I would take Yun to sweep the tomb. Wang Ergu heard about a nearby scenic garden called Guo Garden and asked to visit it together. Seeing the moss-covered rocks with intricate patterns, Yun pointed them out to me, saying, "Using these stacked rocks to create bonsai is even more elegant than the white stones from Xuanzhou." I said, "If they're all like this, it might be hard to find many." Wang Ergu said, "If my sister-in-law likes these stones so much, I'll pick them for you." She immediately borrowed a sack from the tomb watchers and started picking them up like a crane. Every time I said "good" after picking up a stone, she put it in the sack; if I said "not good," she discarded it aside. Before long, Wang Ergu was sweating profusely and came back dragging the sack, saying, "I can't pick anymore; I'm exhausted." As Yun picked, she said, "I heard that to harvest fruits from the mountains, one must rely on the strength of monkeys. It's true." Wang Ergu, frustrated, used her fingers to tickle Yun. I stood between them and scolded Yun, saying, "While others work hard to pick, you sit comfortably and make such remarks. Don't blame my sister for getting angry!" On the way back, we visited Guo Garden. The garden was full of lush greenery and colorful flowers. Wang Ergu, being straightforward, would pluck flowers wherever she went. Yun scolded her, saying, "Without a vase for them to thrive in, and without wearing them in your hair, what's the point of picking so many?" Wang Ergu said, "Flower branches don't feel pain. What harm is there in picking them?" I laughed and said, "In the future, heaven will punish you by marrying a man with a rough face and lots of beard, making you vent your frustration on these flowers." Wang Ergu glared at me, threw the flower branches on the ground, and then used her toes to flick them into the pool, saying angrily, "Why do you have to insult me so much!" Yun smiled and pacified her before things escalated.

When Yun first came to me, she didn't talk much and preferred listening to me speak eloquently. I tried to engage her interests, patiently encouraging her like coaxing a cricket with fine grass until she gradually became more talkative.

Every day at meals, she insisted on using tea to soak rice, enjoyed eating fermented bean curd, which is called "stinky tofu" in Wu dialect, and liked shrimp paste with melon. These were foods I disliked the most, so I teased her, saying, "Dogs have no stomachs, so they eat feces because they don't know its smell and filthiness; dung beetles like to eat dung balls and turn into cicadas, wanting to fly to higher places. Are you a dog or a cicada?" Yun said, "I'm used to eating fermented bean curd since it's cheap and can be eaten with porridge or rice. I've been eating it since I was young. Now that I'm in your house, I've become a dung beetle turning into a cicada, still liking to eat them, just not forgetting where I came from. As for shrimp paste with melon, I only started eating it when I came to your house." I said, "Is my house a dog kennel?" Yun explained embarrassedly, "Every family has their own habits; the only difference is whether they eat it or not. You like to eat garlic, so I reluctantly eat a little too. I won't force you to eat fermented bean curd, but you can try a little shrimp paste with melon while pinching your nose. Once it's in your mouth, you'll know its deliciousness. It's like the story of the Plain Girl from ancient times, ugly in appearance but with beautiful virtues." I laughed and said, "Are you trying to trap me into being a dog?" Yun said, "I've been a dog for a long time; let you taste it too." With that, she picked up a piece of melon with her chopsticks and stuffed it into my mouth. I chewed with my nose covered and found it surprisingly crispy and refreshing. After releasing my nose, I ate a few more pieces and found it to be a rare delicacy. From then on, I also liked eating shrimp paste with melon. Yun also mixed fermented bean curd with sesame oil and a little sugar, which tasted delicious. She mashed the melon with shrimp paste, named it "Double Fresh Sauce," and it tasted unique.

I said, "I initially hated it to the extreme, but in the end, I liked it. The reason behind this is really hard to understand." Yun said, "Love overrides everything, even ugliness isn't a hindrance." I said, "Unfortunately, you're a woman; if you could transform into a man, we could travel together to famous mountains, explore scenic spots, and roam the world, how joyful it would be!" Yun said, "What's so difficult about that? When my hair turns gray, even if I can't travel far to the Five Sacred Mountains, places like Tiger Hill, Lingyan Mountain, West Lake in the south, and Yangzhou in the north would still be enjoyable to visit." I said, "By the time your hair turns gray, your feet might not be convenient anymore." Yun said, "If not in this life, then let's make a wish for the next." I said, "In the next life, you become a man, and I'll be a woman following you." Yun said, "Only by not forgetting this life will it be more interesting."

I said, "The bowl of porridge from childhood has not been fully discussed yet. If we don't forget this life in the next life, on our wedding night, let's talk about our past in detail. Then, there's no need to close our eyes, right?"

Yun said, "It is said that the Matchmaker Deity specializes in earthly marriages. In this life, you and I have become husband and wife, already grateful for his matchmaking. For our next life's marriage fate, we also need to rely on his divine power. Why not paint a small portrait to worship him?"

At that time, there was an artist named Zun from Zhejiang, Taixi, who was skilled in painting figures. So, I asked him to paint one. In the painting, the Matchmaker Deity held a red thread in one hand and a cane in the other, with a marriage book hanging above, and he had both white hair and a youthful appearance, walking in the fairy air without smoke or fog. This painting was Zun's masterpiece. My friend, Stone Zhutang, also wrote a praise at the beginning of the scroll. I hung the painting in the inner room. Every month, on the first and last days of the month, my wife and I burned incense, worshipped, and prayed. Later, due to many changes in the family, this painting was somehow lost.

"His life is unpredictable, this life ends." Can two devoted individuals really receive the protection of the gods?

After moving to Warehouse Rice Lane, I inscribed the plaque on the bedroom loft as "Guest Fragrance Pavilion," taking the meaning of mutual respect from Yun's name. The courtyard was narrow with high walls, lacking in scenery. Behind was a wing leading to the book storage, where you could see the abandoned garden of the Lu family through the window. However, it had a somewhat desolate atmosphere. The scenery of Canglang Pavilion often lingered in Yun's heart.

There was an old woman living east of Jinmu Bridge, north of Geng Lane, with vegetable gardens surrounding her house, woven with fences as gates. Outside the gate was a pond, about an acre in size, with the reflection of flowers and trees shimmering around the fence. This place was the former residence of Zhang Shicheng, the warlord at the end of the Yuan Dynasty. Not far west of the house, there was a mound of rubble, from which you could overlook the distance. The area nearby was deserted, with few people, quite remote and wild.

When the old woman mentioned this place, Yun couldn't forget it and said to me, "Since leaving Canglang Pavilion, I often dream of returning there. Today, we have no choice but to settle for something slightly inferior. Shall we move to live with the old woman?"

I said, "The scorching summer days have been continuous recently, and I was just thinking of finding a cool place to pass the time. If you're willing to go, I'll first see if her house is suitable for living. If it is, we'll bring our luggage and stay there for a month. How about that?"

Yun said, "I'm afraid your mother won't agree."

I said, "I'll persuade her."

The next day, I went to the old woman's place. I found that there were only two rooms in the house, divided into four small rooms front and back. However, with paper windows and bamboo beds, it had a quiet and elegant atmosphere. The old woman knew my intentions and gladly rented her bedroom to us. With white paper pasted on the walls, the room instantly looked refreshed.

So, I informed my mother and moved with Yun.

There was only one old couple living next door, who made a living by growing vegetables. When they heard that we were staying to avoid the summer heat, they came over first to show their respect, bringing pond fish they had caught and vegetables from their garden as gifts. They didn't accept money when I offered it to them. Yun made shoes for them as a gift, which they accepted with gratitude only after some persuasion.

It was July, with lush green shade covering the area, a breeze blowing over the water's surface, and the cicadas chirping loudly. The old couple came to make fishing rods for us, and Yun and I spent the days fishing in the shade of the willows. At sunset, we climbed the earthen mound to watch the sunset and evening glow, composing poems spontaneously, such as "Beasts devouring the setting sun, bows shooting shooting stars."

In the blink of an eye, the moon reflected in the pond, the insects chirped loudly, and we moved the bamboo bed to the side of the fence. At this time, the old woman announced that the wine was warm and the meal was ready. The two of us drank under the moonlight, only starting to eat when we felt tipsy. After bathing, we put on sandals, took banana leaf fans, and sat or lay by the fence, listening to the old neighbors talk about stories of cause and effect. We only returned to the house to sleep at midnight, feeling cool and comfortable all over, almost forgetting that we were living in the city.

I asked the old woman to buy chrysanthemums and planted them along the fence. When the chrysanthemums bloomed in September, Yun and I stayed there for ten days. My mother also happily came to visit, admiring the chrysanthemums and eating crabs, playing all day.

Yun said happily, "In the future, we should live here together. Buy ten acres of vegetable land around the house, hire servants to plant fruits and vegetables for daily expenses. You paint, I embroider, exchanging money for writing poems and drinking. Living a simple life, happily ever after. There's no need to make tiresome travel plans anymore."

I deeply understood her words. Even today, if I have such a beautiful place, my confidant has long since left this world. Among the regrets, even the deepest sighs are hard to dispel from my heart!

Half a mile away from home, there is a Dongting Lord's Temple in Vinegar Warehouse Lane, commonly known as the Narcissus

Temple. The corridors in the temple are winding, with some pavilions. On the birthdays of the immortals, many families in the city each claim a corner, quietly hanging a standardized glass lamp, placing a throne underneath, and arranging vases and flowers for comparison. During the day, it's just a play, but at night, candles of various heights are placed among the flowers, called "Flower Illumination." At this time, the light of flowers and the shadow of lamps shimmer endlessly, with the fragrance of incense lingering over the precious tripod, like a banquet in the Dragon Palace.

The caretakers would either play music with sheng and xiao, or brew tea for a casual chat. The viewers gathered like ants, and even the eaves were fitted with railings as restrictions. I was invited by a friend to come and arrange flowers, so I had the opportunity to witness this grand event. After returning home, I praised the grandeur of the temple festival to Yun. Yun said, "It's a pity I'm not a man and can't go."

I said, "Wear my hat, put on my clothes, and it's a way to disguise as a man."

So, Yun changed her hairstyle to braids, thickened her eyebrows, and put on my hat, only revealing her temples, which could barely conceal her identity. After putting on my clothes, which were an inch and a half too long, they were folded at the waist and sewn, then covered with a horseman's robe. Yun said, "What about the shoes?"

I said, "There's a kind of butterfly shoes on the market, adjustable in size, very convenient to buy, and can also be used as slippers in the morning and evening. Isn't that great?" Yun readily agreed to my suggestion.

After dinner, Yun dressed up and imitated the appearance of a man, practicing for a long time. Suddenly, she changed her mind and said, "I'm not going anymore. If someone recognizes me, it wouldn't be appropriate if your mother found out." I persuaded her, saying, "Who in the temple's management doesn't know me? Even if they recognize us, it will just be a smile. My mother is at my cousin's house, so we'll go quietly and come back quietly. How could she know?"

Yun looked at herself in the mirror, laughed heartily, and I strongly held her arm and quietly went to the Narcissus Temple, visiting all the sights without anyone realizing she was a woman. When someone asked who she was, I answered as my cousin, and she just bowed in return.

Finally, we arrived at a corner where a young woman and a little girl sat behind the throne, the relatives of a man named Yang who managed the temple. Yun suddenly walked over and greeted them, leaning her body slightly and naturally placing her hand on the young woman's shoulder. A maid beside them stood up and scolded, "Who's this rude person?!"

I was about to find an excuse to cover for her, but seeing the situation turn unfavorable, Yun immediately took off her hat and stood on tiptoe to show them, saying, "I'm also a woman."

The people were surprised, then turned from anger to joy, inviting Yun to stay for tea and snacks. Later, they called for a sedan chair to send Yun back home.

Money Master Zhu from Wujiang passed away, and my father wrote back, asking me to offer condolences. Yun privately said to me, "Going to Wujiang will definitely pass through Taihu Lake. I want to go with you and broaden my horizons." I said, "I was worried about traveling alone. Having you with me is, of course, very good, but there's no suitable excuse." Yun said, "Let's say we're going back to my mother's home. You board the boat first, and I'll follow soon after." I said, "In that case, when we come back, we'll stop the boat under the Wanqian Bridge and enjoy the moonlight together, continuing the elegant atmosphere of Canglang Pavilion." It was June 18th at the time.

On this clear morning, with the weather cool, I arrived at Xujing Ferry with a servant and boarded the boat to wait. Before long, Yun arrived in a sedan chair. After untying the ropes and passing Tiger Roar Bridge, we gradually saw the sails and sandpipers, where the water met the sky. Yun said, "Is this the famous Taihu Lake? Today, I finally see the vastness of heaven and earth. It's truly worth it. Think about how many women in their chambers might never see Taihu Lake in their lifetime." Before we could chat much, we had already arrived in Wujiang.

After disembarking and paying my respects, I returned to the boat to find it empty. Worried, I asked the boatman. He pointed and said, "Didn't you see the person watching the fish eagles under the shade of the willow trees by Changqiao Bridge?" It turned out Yun had already gone ashore with the boatman's daughter.

I went behind them, finding Yun flushed with sweat, leaning on the boatman's daughter, lost in thought. I tapped her shoulder and said, "Your clothes are all soaked with sweat."

Yun turned and said, "I was worried about the Qian family

coming onto the boat, so I temporarily avoided it. Why did you come back so soon?"

I laughed and said, "I had to chase a fugitive."

So, the two of us boarded arm in arm and turned the boat towards Wanqian Bridge. The sun had yet to set, and all the windows on the boat were open, with a gentle breeze blowing. Yun held a silk fan, gently stroking her silk robe, while the boatman sliced melons to cool off. Before long, the evening glow tinged the bridge red, dusk enveloped the willows by the river, the moon was about to rise, and the lights of the fishermen had already dotted the river.

I instructed the servant to go to the stern and drink with the boatman. The boatman's daughter was named Suyun, and we had some acquaintance. She called Yun over to sit with her. With no light at the bow, we waited for the moon to rise, using riddles as drinking games, with cups of wine continuously flowing. Suyun's eyes sparkled, and after listening for a while, she said, "I'm quite familiar with drinking games, but I've never heard of this one. Can you teach me?" Yun immediately used a metaphor to enlighten her, but she still seemed confused.

I laughed and said, "Madam, let's pause on the instruction for now. I can explain it clearly with just one metaphor."

Yun asked, "What metaphor do you have?"

I said, "Cranes are good at dancing but cannot plow the fields; oxen are good at plowing but cannot dance. This is due to the nature of things. Trying to teach against the nature of things is futile, isn't it?"

Suyun jokingly punched my shoulder and said, "Are you scolding me?"

Yun set the rules for the drinking game: "You can speak but not touch. Violators must drink a large cup of wine." Suyun had a good tolerance for alcohol and downed a large cup in one gulp.

I said, "You can touch, but only groping. No hitting allowed."

Yun laughed and embraced Suyun, pushing her into my arms, saying, "Feel free to grope as you wish."

I chuckled and said, "You're not very considerate. Groping should be done subtly, almost inadvertently. Embracing and roughly fondling is the behavior of country bumpkins."

At that time, both Yun and Suyun had jasmine branches pinned to their hair, and with the scent of wine, mixed with the sweat and hair oil of women, the fragrance was overwhelming. I teased, "The stench of a peasant fills the bow of the boat, making one nauseous." Suyun couldn't help but punch me repeatedly, saying, "Who told you to sniff around me so brazenly!" Yun called out, "Violation! Violation! Two more cups of wine as punishment." Suyun said, "He insulted me as a peasant, shouldn't I hit him?" Yun said, "When he said 'peasant,' there's a story behind it. Finish the punishment, and I'll tell you the reason." So Suyun downed two more cups of wine. Yun then told her about the cooling-off stories from their time living in Canglang Pavilion. Suyun said, "If that's the case, I've misunderstood. I should be punished again." After saying that, she drank another cup. Yun said, "I've heard that Suyun is skilled in singing. Can we hear her melodious voice?" So Suyun tapped on a small plate with ivory chopsticks and began to sing. Yun also enjoyed herself, drinking and reveling, unknowingly getting very drunk, and then left in a sedan chair. I stayed behind to chat with Suyun for a while before returning home under the moonlight.

At that time, I was staying at my friend Lu Banfang's Xiaoshuang Tower. After several days, Lu's wife mistakenly believed some rumors and quietly said to Yun, "A few days ago, I heard that your husband took two prostitutes to drink and revel on a boat under Wanqian Bridge. Did you know?" Yun said, "There is such a thing. One of those people was me." She then explained the whole story of their trip to visit Taihu Lake in detail. Lu's wife laughed loudly after hearing it, dispelling her doubts and leaving.

In the year of Qianyin (1794), in July, I returned from Guangdong. A companion named Xu Xiufeng brought his concubine back with him. Xiufeng was my cousin-in-law; he flaunted the beauty of his new companion and invited Yun to come and see. After a few days, Yun said to Xiufeng, "She's indeed beautiful, but lacks a bit of charm." Xiufeng said, "So you mean if your husband takes a concubine, she must be both beautiful and charming?" Yun said, "Of course." From then on, she actively searched for concubines for me, but was limited by the lack of funds.

At that time, there was a prostitute named Wen Lengxiang from Zhejiang, residing in Wu, who wrote four poems called "Ode to Willow Catkins," which spread widely in Suzhou City, with many people writing poetry and singing along with her. My friend Zhang Xianhan from Wujiang had always admired Wen Lengxiang and asked me to write poetry to accompany hers. Yun looked down on him and set the poems aside. I felt the urge and wrote several poems following her rhyme scheme, one of which had the line, "My spring sorrow is delicately elegant, his departure is even more entangled." Yun greatly appreciated it.

In the autumn of the following year (1795), on the fifth day of the eighth month, my mother was about to take Yun to visit Tiger Hill when Xianhan suddenly came and said, "I'm also planning a trip to Tiger Hill. Today, I specially invite you to be the envoy of the king." He asked me to meet him at Half Pond at Tiger Hill while letting my mother go ahead.

Xianhan took me to Wen Lengxiang's residence, where we met the somewhat elderly Wen Lengxiang. She had a daughter named Hanyuan, who was not yet sixteen years old, graceful and elegant, a wonderful girl resembling "autumn water reflecting the cold." During the conversation, it was discovered that she was quite knowledgeable in literature and art. She had a younger sister named Wenyuan, who was still very young. At that time, I had no wild thoughts, and besides, I thought that the expenses required for such entertainment were beyond what a poor scholar like me could afford.

However, since I was in such a situation, feeling uneasy in my heart, I could only reluctantly go along with it. I asked Xianhan privately, "I'm just a poor scholar. Are you playing with me with such a rare beauty?" Xianhan laughed and said, "Of course not. Today, a friend invited Hanyuan to thank me, but unfortunately, the host was taken away by a distinguished guest, so I'm here on behalf of the host to invite the guest again. You don't have to worry about anything." I felt relieved after hearing this.

At Half Pond, two boats met, and Hanyuan boarded the other boat to pay respects to my mother. When Yun and Hanyuan met for the first time, it was as if they were old acquaintances. They held hands and climbed the mountain to admire the scenery, visiting many famous spots. Yun particularly loved the height of Qianqingyun and sat there admiring it for a long time. Upon returning to Wild Fragrance Shore, everyone enjoyed drinking and was extremely happy, with both boats docked together.

When it was time to untie the ropes and return, Yun said to me, "You accompany Zhang Jun, and leave Hanyuan to accompany me. How about that?" I agreed to her suggestion. On the return journey passing through Duting Bridge, we each returned to our own boat.

Back at home, it was already the middle of the night. Yun said, "Today, I finally met a beautiful and charming woman. Just now, I made an appointment with Hanyuan. She will come find me tomorrow, and I will definitely find a way for you to get her." I was surprised and said, "This person cannot be kept without a golden house. How could a poor student like me dare to have such wild thoughts? Moreover, we have a deep bond as husband and wife, so why seek outside?" Yun smiled and said, "I also really like her. Just wait patiently for now."

The next day at noon, Hanyuan did indeed come. Yun entertained her warmly. At the banquet, we played guessing games with dice, with winners drinking and losers singing, until the end of the banquet, not a single word of solicitation was spoken.

After Hanyuan left, Yun said, "I just made an appointment with Hanyuan again. She will come here on the 18th to become my sister. It's best for you to prepare some sacrifices." She laughed and pointed to the jade bracelet on her arm, saying, "If you see this bracelet belonging to Hanyuan, then the matter is settled. I've already mentioned the intention to take her as a concubine, but I haven't delved into her inner thoughts yet." I tentatively listened to her words, unsure of the outcome.

On the 18th, it was raining heavily, but Hanyuan still came.

After spending a long time indoors, the two came out holding hands. When I saw that Hanyuan still looked shy, I realized that the jade bracelet was already on her arm. They burned incense and made a covenant, and the originally planned drinking for fun, coinciding with Hanyuan's desire to go play at Shihu Lake, was the end of it.

Yun said to me happily, "The beauty is now in hand. How will you thank the matchmaker?" I asked her for the detailed process, and Yun said, "The reason I spoke quietly earlier was because I was afraid that Hanyuan might have feelings for someone else. I asked her just now, and she doesn't have anyone in her heart. I told her: Does sister understand my intentions today? Hanyuan replied: I am honored by Madam's favor, truly like a weed leaning on a jade tree. But my mother has high hopes for me, and I'm afraid it would be difficult to make decisions on my own. Let's hope we can both think of a solution slowly. When I took off the jade bracelet and put it on her arm, I reminded her again: Jade symbolizes firmness and endless reunion. Try wearing it as a good omen. Hanyuan said: Whether we can be reunited or not depends on Madam's decision." It seems that Hanyuan's heart has already belonged to you. What's difficult to deal with is Wen Lengxiang. We should think of a way again."

I smiled and said, "Are you trying to emulate the plot of Li Yu's 'A Tower for the Lonely Wife'?"

Yun said, "Yes."

From then on, there was not a day that she did not talk about Hanyuan. However, Hanyuan was taken away by someone with power. In the end, things did not go as desired.

Yun eventually died because of this matter.

VOLUME TWO: LEISURE AND PLEASURE

I remember when I was a child, I could stare directly at the sun with wide eyes and see even the smallest things clearly. When I encountered tiny objects, I would carefully observe their texture and structure, often experiencing extraordinary joy. In the summer, the buzzing of mosquitoes sounded like thunder to me, and I would imagine them as a group of cranes dancing in the sky; once this thought entered my mind, thousands of cranes would indeed appear before me. Looking up at them, my neck would become stiff.

I would trap mosquitoes inside a white mosquito net and slowly cover them with smoke, causing them to buzz towards the smoke. In my eyes, they became white cranes in the clouds, singing joyfully like cranes in the sky, which was delightful and commendable.

In the uneven walls and the grassy flower beds, I would often squat down beside them, observing them at the same height as the flower beds, focusing intently. I would imagine the thick grass as a forest, insects as giant beasts, raised mounds as hills, and sunken areas as valleys. I would wander among them in my mind, feeling extremely pleased.

One day, I saw two insects fighting among the grass, completely engrossed in watching, when suddenly a huge creature appeared, looming over them like a giant. It turned out to be a toad, which stretched out its tongue and swallowed both insects whole. At that time, still young, I was so absorbed in watching that I couldn't help but let out a startled scream. Once my mind settled, I caught the toad and whipped it dozens of times before driving it away.

Reflecting on this incident in later years, I realized that the two insects were probably fighting because one was plotting deceit while the other did not comply. As the old saying goes, "Deceitfulness leads to death," and aren't the insects the same? I was fascinated by this joy of observing the grass, to the extent that my genitals were sucked by earthworms, causing swelling and difficulty urinating. A servant caught a duck and let it approach my genitals, opening its mouth to suck out the poison of the earthworms. Suddenly, the servant let go, and the duck abruptly lifted its neck, looking as if it was going to swallow, frightening me into crying uncontrollably, and it became a topic of conversation thereafter.

These are the leisurely pastimes of my childhood.

As I grew older, I developed a passion for flowers and bonsai. But it wasn't until I met Zhang Lanpo that I mastered the art of pruning and nurturing bonsai, and then understood the secrets of grafting flowers and stacking stones. Lanpo was fond of orchids, primarily because of their rare and elegant fragrance. As for petal quality, those that were somewhat suitable for flower charts were even more rare. Before Lanpo passed away, he gifted me a pot of spring orchids with lotus petals, its shoulders broad and heart wide, its stem slender and petals pure, worthy of inclusion in a flower chart, and I treasured it like a precious gem.

While I was traveling, Yun personally watered it, and the leaves flourished. However, in less than two years, it suddenly withered and died. Upon pulling it up to inspect the roots, they were as white as jade, and the flower buds were full of vitality. Initially, I couldn't understand the reason behind it and thought that I was not fortunate enough to appreciate it, so I could only sigh. It was not until much later that I learned that someone wanted to separate a pot from it, and when I refused, that person poured boiling water over it, killing it. Since then, I vowed never to raise orchids again.

Among flowers, the second favorite is azalea. Although it has no fragrance, its flowers can be enjoyed for a long time, and it is easy to prune. However, due to Yun's care for the branches and leaves, I couldn't bear to trim them, so it was difficult to grow them into large trees. The same goes for other bonsai.

Only during the blooming of chrysanthemums in autumn do I feel a surge of autumnal inspiration. I enjoy picking flowers and arranging them in vases rather than planting them in pots. It's not that potted plants are not enjoyable to behold, but because there is no garden at home and no place to plant them personally, buying them from the market results in disorderly and ungraceful arrangements, so I'd rather not play with potted plants.

In flower arranging, the number of flower branches should preferably be odd, not even. Each vase should contain only one type of flower branch, not two different colors. The mouth of the vase should be wide and large, not narrow; only then can the flower branches be inserted smoothly and naturally. Whether it's five branches or seven branches, or thirty or forty branches, there must be a clump of branches rising in the middle of the mouth of the vase, with a slight tilt, not centered and upright; it's best if it's neither scattered nor squeezed together, nor too close to the mouth of the vase. This is what experts call "properly rising."

As for the shape of the flower branches, whether they stand tall and straight or dance diagonally, they should be irregularly arranged, and flower racks can be used to space them out to avoid the pitfall of appearing cluttered like a "flying plate." The leaves of the flower branches should not be disorderly, the flower stems should not be too hard, and the connecting pins should be hidden, with the pins preferably cut short rather than exposed outside the stem; this is what experts call "clear mouth."

Depending on the size of the table, three to seven vases of flowers can be placed on a table. If there are too many, it will appear cluttered, like the chrysanthemum barriers in common households. The height of the tables should range from three to four inches to two or three feet, with uneven heights, arranged in a staggered and harmonious manner, complementing each other, for the best aesthetic appeal. If the middle is higher than the sides, or the back is higher than the front, lined up in rows, it would fall into the deliberate and unnatural flaw called "tapestry pile."

The flower arrangements in vases, whether dense or sparse, the arrangement of tables, whether advancing or retreating, all depends on whether the person who understands the beauty of creation can arrange them as if in a painting to be considered qualified.

If using pots, bowls, plates, or basins, you can first mix alum, pine resin, elm bark, flour, and oil, and boil them into a glue. Thread copper plates onto nails, with the tips facing upwards, then melt the glue with fire, and stick the copper plates onto the pots, bowls, plates, or basins. After cooling, insert the flower branches into the nails with iron wire tied into a bunch, inserting them into the nails at a slight angle, not centered and upright; it's best if the flower bundle is sparse and slender, not crowded. At this point, add water and bury the copper plates with a little fine sand, making it appear as if the flower cluster is growing at the bottom of the bowl, which is considered excellent.

For wooden flower and fruit arrangements, the method of pruning (not being able to personally search for every type of flower branch, often resulting in dissatisfaction) must first be grasped in the hand and observed from both horizontal and oblique angles to determine its posture, and then select its form from the reverse and side angles. After selecting the desired form, trim off the messy branches to highlight its sparse, thin, ancient, and unique qualities.

Next, consider how to insert the branch into the vase. Whether breaking or bending, insert it into the mouth of the vase to avoid the hassle of the back of the leaf and the side of the flower. If holding a single branch, insert the straight stem into the vase first, the posture will inevitably be messy and the stem strong, with the back of the leaf and the side of the flower, making it difficult to select the surface posture and lacking in charm. The method of breaking and bending the stem involves sawing off half of the stem and embedding it with bricks and stones. In this way, even the straight stem will have a curved posture. If worried about the stem tipping over, drive in one or two nails to secure it. With this method, even maple leaves and bamboo branches, wild grass and thorns can be used as materials for flower arrangements. For example, with a green bamboo pole, paired with a few wolfberry fruits; or a few stalks of thin grass paired with two thorns. If positioned properly, it will have an extraordinary and refined charm.

For newly planted trees, they can be positioned slantingly, allowing them to grow towards the side of the pot, and after a year, the branches and leaves will naturally grow upwards. If every tree is planted straight, it will be difficult to achieve a good posture.

As for pruning bonsai, first select the roots that resemble chicken claws, cut them into three sections from left to right, then start the branches. One branch per section, seven branches to the top, or nine branches to the top. Care must be taken to avoid shoulder-like knots on the branches, and the joints should not be as swollen as crane knees. The branches must spiral out, not just left and right, to avoid the flaw of "bare chest and exposed back"; but they should also not sprout straight forward and backward. There is a saying in the industry called "double rising" or "triple rising," which means planting one tree root and cultivating two or three trees from it. If the root is not shaped like chicken claws, it becomes a straight-planted tree, so such root sections are not selected.

However, it takes at least thirty to forty years for a single bonsai to be pruned into shape. In my lifetime, I have only seen Mr. Wan Caizhang, a fellow villager, prune a few trees. And at a shop in

Yangzhou, I saw a gift from tourists to Yushan, a pot of boxwood and a pot of green cypress, but unfortunately, it was like casting pearls before swine, as I did not see them being cherished. If the pruned branches of a bonsai are twisted like pagodas and the fixed branches are bent like earthworms, it becomes a craftsman's bonsai.

Flower and stone embellishments in bonsai, small scenes can be painted, and large scenes can be wandered in. A cup of clear tea can immerse one in contemplation, allowing for refined appreciation in the quiet chamber.

Without Lingbi stones for planting narcissus, I tried using charcoal with the meaning of rocks instead. The tender heart of the yellow sprout vegetable, as white as jade, is selected in sizes of five or six, planted in a rectangular pot with sand, and then replaced with charcoal instead of stones, contrasting black and white, quite elegant. By combining similar materials, there is endless charm and it's difficult to describe them all.

For example, chewing on the seeds of water iris with cold rice soup, spraying them on charcoal, and placing them in a damp place will grow delicate iris flowers; then transplant them into pots or bowls at will, and they will be lovely with lush greenery.

Grind the ends of old lotus seeds thin, place them in eggshells, let the mother hen incubate them, and when the young shoots grow out, take them out, then crush aged swallow's nest mud with a few pieces of Tianmendong's rhizome, mix well, and plant the young lotus seedlings in small containers, watering them with river water, and bathing them in sunlight in the morning; soon after, when the flowers bloom, the flowers will be as large as wine cups, but the leaves will shrink to the size of bowl mouths, exceedingly lovely.

In arranging garden pavilions and towers, or in constructing winding corridors and stacking stones to form mountains, or in planting flowers to create scenic views, attention must be paid to the principle of seeing the large within the small, and the small within the large, with a balance of solidity and emptiness, concealment and exposure, shallowness and depth. The subtlety lies not only in the phrase "winding and twisting" but also in the abundance of the land and stones; otherwise, it would merely be a waste of effort and resources. For example, digging and piling up soil to form a mountain, then scattering large stones on top and interspersing them with flowers and plants, using plum trees as fences and vine trees as walls. In this way, even if there is no real mountain, one can create the illusion of a mountain.

The principle of seeing the large within the small means, for instance, planting bamboo in open and flat areas where it grows easily, using lush plum trees to weave fences as barriers. The principle of seeing the small within the large means, for example, designing the walls of narrow courtyards to have undulating surfaces, decorating the walls with greenery, planting vines in the corners, embedding large stones in the walls, and carving inscriptions or drawings on them. When looking out the window, it will give the impression of steepness and openness. The principle of having solidity within emptiness means, for example, at the end of a rockery pond, there is a sudden openness after a turn; or, in a pavilion or room, there is a dining area that opens into another courtyard when the door is opened. The principle of having emptiness within solidity means, for example, having a door that leads to a nonexistent courtyard, but instead, there is a false door hidden among bamboo and stones, creating the illusion of a door that doesn't exist; or, setting up low railings on top of a wall, creating the impression of a terrace, even though there is no actual terrace.

For those with limited means and crowded households, they should follow the example of the rear cabin of the Tai Ping boat in my hometown, but with some modifications. The central steps can be used as beds, arranged closely together to accommodate three beds; then, wooden boards can be used to divide the space, pasting them with paper, thus separating the space vertically and horizontally. Understanding this method, it's as if walking along an endless road, without feeling its narrowness. When my wife and I lived in Yangzhou, we followed this method. At that time, our house had only two rooms, but by partitioning them off for bedrooms, kitchen, and living room, the space still seemed more than adequate. My wife once laughed and said, "Although this arrangement is exquisite, it doesn't quite give off the air of a wealthy household."

Indeed, that was the case!

Once, when I was sweeping the graves in the mountains, I found stones with mountain-like patterns. I discussed with my wife, Yun, saying, "People use oil and lime to stack stones from Xuanzhou on white stone basins because their colors harmonize well. Although the local yellow stones are quaint, if we were to use oil and lime to connect them, the yellow and white colors would mix, and the traces of carving would be completely exposed. What should we do?"

Yun said, "Select some inferior yellow stones, grind them into powder, and smear them on the areas connected with oil and lime while they are still wet. After drying, the colors may match." So, I followed her advice and used a rectangular basin from Yixing to stack a rockery. With a slope on the left and a protrusion on the right, the back had horizontal stone patterns, resembling the method of Yunlin stone, with rugged peaks and valleys, like riverside cliffs. In one corner, I planted a thousand-petal white water lily, while on top of the rockery, I planted navel-wort, also known as cloud pine.

After several days of work, it was finally completed.

In deep autumn, the navel-wort spread over the entire mountain, resembling vines hanging on a cliff, with flowers in bright red and white water lilies blooming on the surface of the water, creating a mix of red and white. Walking among them, it felt like stepping onto the fairyland of Penglai. Placing the rockery under the eaves, Yun and I admired and evaluated it together: here, we could set up a water pavilion; there, we could build a thatched pavilion; here, we could carve six characters: "Between Falling Flowers and Flowing Water"; here, we could live; here, we could fish; here, we could enjoy the distant view. With countless ideas in mind, it felt as if we were about to move into this rockery.

One evening, while two cats were fighting over food, they fell from the eaves, breaking all the pots and stands in an instant. I sighed and said, "Even such a small thing has offended the Creator?" Both Yun and I couldn't help but shed tears of sadness.

Burning incense in a quiet room is a refined pleasure during leisure time.

Yun once steamed aloeswood, benzoin, and other incense in a rice cooker until they were thoroughly heated, then placed a copper wire rack about half an inch away from the flame on the stove, slowly roasting them. At this time, the fragrance was subtle and profound, without any smoke.

Buddha's hand fruit should not be smelled by those who are drunk, as it tends to rot easily after being smelled. Papaya should not come into contact with sweat; if it does, it should be washed with water. Only yuzu has no such prohibitions. There are also methods of offering Buddha's hand fruit and papaya, but I won't elaborate on them here.

Whenever someone casually takes down the arranged offerings to smell them and then puts them aside, it shows that they don't understand the proper way of offering.

During my leisure time, there were always flower vases on the table.

Yun said, "Your flower arrangements capture the essence of the weather and seasons; they are truly exquisite. In painting, there is often the method of meticulously depicting insects. Why not try to imitate this?"

I said, "But insects jump and move unpredictably; how can we imitate them?"

Yun said, "I have a method, but it may involve the sin of using living creatures as decorations."

I asked her to explain.

Yun said, "After insects die, their colors remain unchanged. Find some mantises, cicadas, butterflies, etc., pierce them with a needle to kill them, then tie a fine thread around their necks and hang them among the flowers and plants. Adjust their limbs so that they appear lifelike, as if they were alive. Isn't this a good idea?"

I was delighted to hear this and followed her method to create insect-themed flower arrangements. Those who saw them were all amazed. Even if I were to ask the ladies in the inner chambers today, I'm afraid they wouldn't have such subtle thoughts.

When my wife and I were staying with the Hua family in Xishan, Mrs. Hua asked her two daughters to learn to read from Yun.

Living in the countryside, the courtyard was spacious, and the summer sun was scorching. Yun taught them how to make "living flower screens," which was quite ingenious. Each flower screen was made of two branches of wood, about four or five inches long, fashioned into the shape of a low stool, with an empty space in the middle. Four horizontal bars were installed, each about one foot wide, with round holes drilled at the four corners, into which bamboo lattice squares were inserted, making the screen about six or seven feet tall. Then, bean plants were grown in sandpots and placed in the screen, allowing the vines to climb and cover it. Two people could move it around. By making several flower screens, they could be arranged as desired, creating the illusion of a screen full of greenery. These screens, with their ventilation and sun-blocking capabilities, flexibility, and ease of replacement, were called "living flower screens." With this method, all kinds of climbing plants and herbs could be used anywhere.

It was indeed a good method for escaping the summer heat in

rural life!

    My friend Lu Banfang, whose style name was Zha, and sobriquet Chunshan, was skilled in painting pine and cypress trees, as well as plum blossoms and chrysanthemums. He was also proficient in clerical script and seal engraving. I stayed in his Xiao Shuang Tower for a year and a half.

    The tower had a total of five rooms, facing east from west, with three rooms where we resided. We could enjoy the view in the morning and evening, as well as during windy and rainy times. There was a magnolia tree in the courtyard, emitting a refreshing fragrance. The environment was extremely quiet, with corridors and side rooms. When I moved in, I brought along a servant and an old woman, as well as their young daughter. The servant could make clothes, and the old woman could spin. So, Yun did embroidery, the old woman wove fabric, and the servant made clothes, providing for our daily needs.

    I was always hospitable and would always propose drinking games when serving alcohol. Yun was skilled in cooking with minimal ingredients, and her dishes, made from vegetables, melons, fish, and shrimp, were delicious. Knowing that I wasn't wealthy, friends who visited often contributed money for wine before engaging in discussions all day. I also liked cleanliness, so the floor was always clean, and there were no constraints or restraints. At that time, there were Yang Bufan, whose style name was Changxu, who excelled in portraiture; Yuan Shaoqian, whose style name was Pei, who was proficient in landscapes; and Wang Xinglan, whose style name was Yan, who was skilled in painting flowers and feathers. They also enjoyed the elegant environment of Xiao Shuang Tower and brought their painting materials with them. I learned painting, calligraphy, and seal engraving from them, and the fees I earned from writing were handed over to Yun to prepare tea and wine for guests. Thus, we spent our days without rest, discussing poetry and paintings.

    There were also Xia Dan'an and Xia Yishan, the two brothers, as well as Miao Shanyin and Miao Zhibai, the two brothers, and the ladies Jiang Yunxiang, Lu Juxiang, Zhou Xiaoxia, Guo Xiaoyu, Hua Xingfan, and Zhang Xianhan. They all came and went like swallows on a beam, without any formality. Yun would serve tea and wine gracefully, without revealing any emotions, seizing every opportunity to enjoy the beautiful moments. Today, everyone is scattered, like clouds dispersed, and with the loss of my wife, all those past events are too painful to recall.

There were four taboos in Xiao Shuang Tower: discussing official positions and promotions, talking about government affairs, writing in the Eight-Legged essay style, and gambling or playing dice. Those who violated these taboos had to drink five jin of wine as punishment. There were also four advocated principles: generosity and magnanimity, elegance and refinement, unconventionality, and tranquility and silence.

On a hot summer day with nothing to do, we decided to hold a poetry contest. There were eight participants in each contest, each bringing two hundred copper coins. We drew lots to determine the order, with the person who drew the first lot becoming the main examiner and sitting on the side to invigilate; the person who drew the second lot was responsible for transcribing and could also take their seat. The remaining participants acted as examinees, each going to the transcription area to collect a piece of paper and stamp it with a seal. The main examiner would then provide a five-character or seven-character phrase for each participant, and the participants would have to compose a couplet based on the phrase within a set time, during which they could walk around or stand but were not allowed to whisper to one another. Once the couplets were written, they were placed in a box before the participants took their seats. After all the participants had submitted their work, the person responsible for transcription would open the box, copy the couplets onto a scroll, and present it to the main examiner to prevent any favoritism.

Out of the sixteen couplets, three sets of seven-character triplets and three sets of five-character triplets were selected. The person who ranked first in the triplets became the next main examiner, while the second-ranked person became the transcriber. Those who failed to have either of their couplets selected were fined twenty coins, those with only one selected were fined ten coins, and those who exceeded the time limit faced double punishment. At the end of each contest, the main examiner earned over a hundred coins. We could hold up to ten contests in a day, accumulating thousands of coins over time, providing more than enough money for wine. However, there was an exception for Yun; she was appointed as the official examiner, allowing her to sit and contemplate the test questions.

Yang Bufan once painted a portrait of my wife and me planting flowers, capturing our likeness. On that evening, the moonlight was beautiful, and the shadows of the orchids were cast on the pink wall, creating a serene atmosphere. After drinking, Xing Lan, feeling inspired, said, "Bufan can paint your portraits, and I can paint the shadows of flowers." I chuckled and said, "Can flower shadows resemble human shadows?"

Xing Lan took out a piece of white paper and spread it on the wall, then used ink to draw the shadows of the orchids with varying intensity. When viewed in daylight, although it didn't form a complete painting, the sparse and scattered flowers and leaves had their own charm under the moonlight. Yun treasured this small painting greatly, and everyone inscribed poems on it.

In Suzhou, there are two places called Nan Yuan and Bei Yuan. When the rapeseed flowers were in bloom, we lamented the lack of a tavern to enjoy wine. Some suggested finding a nearby tavern, while others proposed returning after viewing the flowers to drink. However, nothing seemed as enjoyable as drinking hot wine while admiring the flowers.

After much debate, Yun said, "Tomorrow, everyone just needs to contribute money for wine, and I will take care of the stove myself." Everyone agreed with enthusiasm.

After they left, I asked her, "Are you really going to handle the stove yourself?"

Yun replied, "Of course not. I saw someone selling wontons at the market, and he has his own pot and stove. Why don't we hire him? I'll prepare the wine and food in advance, and when we get there, we'll just heat them up. That way, we'll have tea and wine ready."

I said, "While the wine and food are convenient, we still lack tea-making utensils."

Yun said, "I'll bring a clay pot with me. We'll use an iron fork to hang the pot handle and remove the pot from the stove. Then, we'll hang the clay pot over the stove and add firewood to boil tea. Isn't that convenient?" I applauded her ingenuity.

There was a man named Bao selling wontons on the street, so we hired him for a hundred coins to handle the stove and pot. We agreed to meet the next afternoon. Bao readily agreed. The next day, when the flower viewers arrived, I explained the plan to them, and everyone admired Yun's cleverness. After lunch, we set off together, bringing cushions with us. When we arrived at Nan Yuan, we found a shady spot under the willow trees and sat in a circle. We brewed tea first, then, after drinking tea, proceeded to warm the wine and food.

It was a beautiful day, with golden hues everywhere, and people in green and red walking along the paths in the fields. Butterflies and bees were flying around, making us feel intoxicated without drinking. Soon, the wine and food were ready, and we sat on the grass to enjoy the feast. Bao, the wonton seller, also joined us and drank with us. Passersby envied our creative ideas. As the drinking continued and the plates were emptied, some sat, some lay down, some sang, and some recited poetry. As the sun began to set, I longed for the taste of porridge, so Bao immediately bought rice and cooked porridge. After everyone had their fill, we returned home.

Yun asked, "Did you enjoy today's outing?" Everyone replied, "If it weren't for Madam's cleverness, we wouldn't have had such a delightful time!" Everyone laughed and dispersed.

The lifestyle, clothing, food, utensils, and housing of the poor should be frugal and elegant. The method of frugality is to "consider each matter separately."

I like to drink light wine and don't care for many dishes. Yun designed a plum blossom box for me: six small white porcelain plates, each two inches in size, were arranged around one in the center to resemble a plum blossom. They were painted with gray paint, and their shape resembled a plum blossom. With grooves left on both the bottom and the lid, the handle on the lid resembled a flower stem. Placing it on the table, it looked like an ink plum blossom covering the surface. Upon opening the lid, it appeared as if the dishes were arranged in the petals of a plum blossom. With six different colors in one box, two or three close friends could enjoy them freely, adding more when finished. Additionally, a low-rimmed circular plate was made for convenience in placing wine glasses, chopsticks, and wine pots. It could be placed anywhere, making it easy to move around and arrange. This was also a part of frugal dining.

My hats, collars, and socks were all made by Yun herself. When clothes tore, they were mended with pieces from other garments to ensure they were always clean and tidy. The colors of the clothes were chosen to be dim to avoid showing stains. They were suitable for both social occasions and daily wear. This was also a part of frugal dressing.

When I first arrived at Xiao Shuang Tower, I found the lighting too dim, so I used white paper to cover the walls, brightening up the room. In the summer, the windows downstairs were removed, and there were no railings, making me feel exposed and unprotected.

Yun suggested, "Why not use the old bamboo curtains to replace the railing?"

I asked, "How do we do that?"

Yun said, "Use a few dark bamboo poles vertically and horizontally, leaving space for walking. Hang the split bamboo curtain on the horizontal bamboo poles, draping it to the ground at the same height as the table, and secure it with four short bamboo poles in the middle using hemp thread. Then, at the place where the curtain hangs on the horizontal bamboo poles, find some old black cloth strips and wrap them around the bamboo poles together, sewing them up. This way, it serves as both a barrier and decoration without spending money." This is also a method of "considering each matter separately." Similarly, the ancient saying that bamboo scraps and wood chips are useful is indeed true.

In the summer, when the lotus flowers first bloomed, they would hold the buds at night and open them in the morning. Yun would put some tea leaves in small gauze bags and place them in the hearts of the flowers. The next morning, she would take them out and brew them with rainwater, creating an exceptionally delightful aroma.

VOLUME THREE: TROUBLES AND SORROWS

Where do the hardships in life come from? Often, they arise from one's own wrongdoing.

However, my troubles were not caused by my own actions. My character values friendship and honesty, but these traits have burdened me. Moreover, my father, Jia Fugong, is generous and heroic, always helping others in need and supporting various causes. He spends money freely, mostly for the sake of others. My wife and I sometimes had urgent financial needs and had to pawn our belongings to get by. Initially, it was manageable, but soon it became unsustainable. As the saying goes, "Family affairs require money." Initially, there were malicious gossip and later ridicule from family members. "A woman without talent is virtuous," truly a timeless maxim!

Although I am the eldest son, I rank third in the family hierarchy, so everyone at home calls Yun "Third Sister." Later, this changed to "Madam Third." Initially, it was just a playful nickname, but it became a habit, and regardless of seniority, everyone referred to her as "Madam Third." Could this be a sign of impending change in the family?

In the year of Qianlong Yisi (1785), I accompanied my father to serve at the government office in Haining.

Yun attached a note she wrote in a letter to me. After seeing it, my father said, "Since your wife can write, let her write the family letters from now on." Later, when there were some gossip at home, my mother suspected Yun's letters were inappropriate, so she stopped letting her write. When my father saw letters not in Yun's handwriting, he asked me, "Is your wife sick?" I immediately wrote to Yun, but received no reply. After some time, my father angrily said, "It seems your wife no longer cares to write letters!"

When I returned home and inquired about the matter, wanting

to defend her, Yun hastily stopped me, saying, "It's better to be scolded by father-in-law than disliked by mother-in-law." She didn't even attempt to explain herself.

In the spring of the year Gengxu (1790), I served at the government office in Hanjiang.

My father fell ill in Hanjiang, and when I went to visit, I fell ill too. My younger brother, Qitang, was also there to accompany our father. Yun wrote to me, saying, "Qitang once borrowed money from a neighbor woman and asked me to be the guarantor. Now the woman is pressing for repayment." I asked Qitang, who denied knowing anything about it. So, in my reply, I said, "Both father and son are sick now, and there's no money to repay debts. When Qitang returns, he can handle it himself."

In a few days, both my father and I recovered. I returned to the government office in Zhenzhou. Yun's letter happened to arrive in Hanjiang, and when my father opened it, he read about Qitang's borrowing incident and said, "Your mother thinks the old man's illness was caused by the concubine surnamed Yao. Now that the old man's illness is basically cured, it's best to secretly instruct Yao to make excuses to go home, and I'll arrange for her parents to come to Yangzhou to take her back. This is a way for both parties to avoid blame."

My father, furious upon reading the letter, questioned Qitang about borrowing money from a neighbor woman. Qitang denied it, so my father wrote to me, reprimanding me, saying, "Your wife borrowed money behind your back and slandered your younger brother. Moreover, she refers to your mother as 'Lady,' and your father as 'Old Man,' which is absurd! I've arranged for someone to bring her back to Suzhou. If you still have a shred of conscience, you should acknowledge your wrongdoing!"

Receiving this letter was like a bolt from the blue. I immediately wrote back to confess my faults. Then, I borrowed a horse and hurried back to Suzhou, extremely worried that Yun might do something reckless. Upon arriving home and explaining the situation, my family also brought a letter of dismissal from my father, detailing Yun's various wrongdoings, showing extreme coldness. Yun cried and said to me, "I should not have spoken recklessly, but your father should forgive a woman's ignorance." A few days later, my father sent another letter, saying, "I won't do anything extreme. Take your wife and move elsewhere. I don't want to see her, and that will be enough to appease me."

So, I arranged for Yun to stay with relatives. However, she felt uncomfortable living with her maternal family, especially since her mother had passed away and her brother was absent. Fortunately, my friend Lu Banfang heard about our situation and kindly allowed us to stay in his Xiao Shuang Tower.

Two years later, my father finally learned the whole story. Just as I returned from Lingnan, my father personally visited Xiao Shuang Tower and said to Yun, "I know everything now. Would you like to come back home?" We gladly agreed and moved back home to live with my parents. Little did we know that more troubles were to follow with Han Yuan!

Yun has always suffered from a blood disorder, aggravated by the departure of her brother from home and the subsequent death of her mother, Mrs. Jin, due to longing for her son. Since meeting Han Yuan, her condition had not recurred for over a year, and I thought she had found a remedy. However, Han Yuan was taken away by a wealthy man who offered a large sum as a bride price and promised to support his mother. The beauty had become someone else's possession! I learned of this, but I didn't dare to tell Yun.

It wasn't until Yun went to inquire herself that she learned the outcome. She returned in tears, saying to me, "I never expected Han Yuan to be so heartless!"

I said, "You were too sentimental. What emotions can one have in a brothel? Besides, those who desire luxury may not be content with ordinary life. It's better to avoid future regrets than to mourn today."

I comforted her repeatedly, but Yun still harbored resentment for being deceived by Han Yuan, which worsened her illness. She became so weak that she could barely walk, and the medicines were ineffective. Her condition fluctuated, leaving her emaciated and frail. Within a few years, our debts grew, and criticisms at home turned into grievances day by day. My parents, increasingly resentful of Yun for becoming sisters with a courtesan, grew to dislike her more each day. I tried to mediate, but my heart was no longer in the human world.

Yun bore a daughter named Qingjun, who was fourteen years old, intelligent, and capable. Qingjun took charge of pawning jewelry and clothes, which was a great help. She also bore a son named Fengsen, who was twelve years old and studying with a teacher.

For several years, I didn't work at the government office and instead opened a shop selling paintings and calligraphy. The income from three days couldn't cover a day's expenses, causing great distress. In the severe winter, lacking warm clothing, we had to endure. Qingjun shivered due to the thin clothes but insisted she wasn't cold. Therefore, Yun refused to seek medical treatment.

Occasionally, when she could get out of bed, a friend of mine, Zhou Chunxu, returned from the Prince's government in Fuzhou, asking for a copy of the Heart Sutra to be embroidered. Yun thought embroidering sutras could bring blessings and, considering the payment, decided to do it. However, Zhou was in a hurry and couldn't wait long. Yun finished it in just ten days. Her health, already fragile, worsened from the sudden exertion. Not only are those destined to suffer from misfortune, but even the Buddha cannot show mercy!

After finishing the sutra, Yun's condition deteriorated further. She needed care and medication daily, causing resentment among the household.

A man from Shanxi rented the room next to my shop and engaged in usury. He often commissioned me for paintings, allowing us to become acquainted. One day, a friend borrowed fifty taels of silver from him and asked me to guarantee it. Reluctantly, I agreed, but the friend absconded with the money. The man from Shanxi came to me demanding repayment. Initially, I used paintings and calligraphy to settle the debt, but eventually, I had nothing left to repay.

At the end of the year, my father was living at home. The man from Shanxi came to demand payment again, roaring loudly at the doorstep. Upon hearing this, my father called me over and reprimanded me, saying, "We are a respectable family, how could we owe such debts to lowlifes!" I was trying to explain when Yun's childhood sworn sister, who had married and moved to Wuxi, sent someone to inquire about her condition. My father, thinking it was someone sent by Han Yuan, became even angrier, saying, "Your wife disregards proper conduct and is sworn sisters with a courtesan! You also lack ambition, associating freely with lowlifes! If I were to treat you harshly, I would be reluctant; I'll give you three days to quickly find a solution. After this deadline, I'll surely report your unfilial conduct to the authorities!"

Upon hearing the news, Yun cried and said, "It's all my fault if father is so angry. If I were to die, leaving you alone, you would surely feel unbearable guilt; if I stayed, but you avoided me, you would surely feel reluctant. For now, quietly call someone from the Hua family over, and I'll reluctantly ask them about it."

So, Qingjun helped Yun to the door and called someone from the Hua family, asking, "Did your mistress specifically send you, or did you come here on your own?"

The person from the Hua family replied, "Our mistress heard that Madam was bedridden and wanted to come to Suzhou to visit, but she never visited before and didn't want to be presumptuous. Before leaving, she instructed me: if Madam doesn't mind staying in the countryside and feels neglected, she can come to the countryside for recuperation, fulfilling the promise we made as young girls under the lamplight."

It turned out that before Yun and Hua Madam got married, they had made a vow to support each other in sickness. So Yun instructed the person from the Hua family, "Thank you for your trouble. Please hurry back and inform your mistress. Ask her to arrange for a boat to come secretly in two days."

After the person from the Hua family left, Yun said to me, "My sworn sister from the Hua family has deeper feelings than blood relatives. If you agree to go to her house, we might as well go together. But it's inconvenient to bring the children along. It's not suitable to leave them here and trouble our parents. We must settle them within two days."

At that time, I had a cousin named Wang Jingchen, who had a son named Yunshi and wanted to marry Qingjun. Yun said, "I heard that Wang Lang is timid and incompetent, just a conservative person, and the Wang family has no significant assets to inherit. Fortunately, they are a family of poetry and rituals, and they only have one son. Marrying Qingjun to him should be acceptable."

I said to my cousin Jingchen, "My father and you have a nephew-uncle relationship. If you want to marry Qingjun, I think he won't disagree. But when Qingjun grows up and marries into your family, the situation may change. When my wife and I went to Xishan, my cousin informed my parents and let Qingjun be a child bride first. What do you think?"

My cousin Jingchen happily agreed, "I'll follow your arrangement."

As for Fengsen, I entrusted my friend Xia Yishan to recommend him to a shop as an apprentice.

After settling everything, the boat from the Hua family arrived just in time. It was the 25th day of the twelfth lunar month of the Gengshen year (1800).

Yun said, "Leaving alone like this will not only invite ridicule from the neighbors but also the man from Shanxi won't let us go easily. We must leave quietly at five in the morning tomorrow."

I said, "You are still ill. Can you withstand the morning cold?"

Yun said, "Life and death are fated. I don't want to think too much."

We quietly informed my father, and he also thought it was appropriate. That night, we packed half of our belongings onto the boat in advance and let Fengsen lie down first. Qingjun cried beside Yun, and Yun instructed her, saying, "Your mother has suffered so much and is so devoted. Encountering such hardships, fortunately, your father treated me very well. You don't have to worry too much about this trip. Within two or three years, our whole family will surely reunite. After you arrive at your uncle's house, remember to be a good wife and not be like your mother. Your grandfather and grandmother are honored to have you as their daughter-in-law and will surely treat you well. Take all the belongings left behind. Your brother is still young, so I didn't tell him. Tell him before we leave that we are going to see a doctor and will be back in a few days. After we and your father are far away, tell him the reasons, then inform your grandfather."

There was an old woman who knew us from before, the one who rented us her house for summer vacation, willing to accompany us to the countryside, so she was by our side, wiping tears constantly.

It was almost five in the morning. We warmed some porridge and ate tearfully together. Yun forced a smile and said, "In the past, a bowl of porridge brought us together for a lifetime, but today, a bowl of porridge separates mother and child. If one were to write a legend, it could be called 'The Porridge Chronicles.'"

When Fengsen heard the noise, he got up and asked, "Mother, where are you going?"

Yun said, "We're just going to see the doctor."

Fengsen asked, "Why so early?"

Yun replied, "The journey is long. Take care of your sister at home, and don't bother your grandmother. Your father and I will go together and will be back in a few days."

At the crowing of the rooster, Yun, supported by the old woman, stepped out of the back door. Fengsen suddenly cried out, "Mother, you're not coming back!" Qingjun, worried about waking the neighbors, hurriedly covered his mouth to comfort him.

At that moment, Yun and I were heartbroken and couldn't say a word of comfort, just repeating, "Don't cry, don't cry."

After Qingjun closed the door, Yun walked a dozen steps out of the alley, already too tired to walk, so she asked the old woman to carry the lantern, and I carried Yun on my back to continue forward. When we were about to reach the boat, we were almost detained by patrolling guards. Fortunately, the old woman said Yun was her sick daughter, and I was her son-in-law, and the boatmen were all workers from the Hua family who would come to assist upon hearing the sound, so we were allowed to board with their help. After the boat set sail, Yun burst into tears.

From that moment on, mother and son were forever separated!

Hua Madam's husband's name was Dacheng, and they lived in the east of Gaoshan, Wuxi, facing the mountains, earning a living through farming, and they were extremely simple and honest people. His wife, Xia, was Yun's sworn sister.

At the time of noon and afternoon, we finally arrived at the Hua family's house. Hua Madam was already waiting at the door, bringing her two young daughters to the side of the boat. The two women met each other with great joy. With the help of Hua Madam, Yun stepped ashore, and she was warmly welcomed. The women and children around swarmed into the room to watch Yun, some came to greet her, some looked at her with pity, whispering to each other, and the room was filled with the sound of conversation.

Yun said to Hua Madam, "Today feels like a fisherman entering the Peach Blossom Spring."

Hua Madam said, "Don't be laughed at, sister. Country folks are just not used to seeing strangers."

From then on, my wife and I lived as guests in Xishan, peacefully celebrating the Spring Festival.

By the Lantern Festival, we had only been in the countryside of Xishan for less than two months, and Yun was gradually able to get out of bed and walk. On that night, we watched the dragon lanterns in the wheat field, and her complexion and spirits gradually recovered. My heart settled a bit, and I privately discussed with her, saying, "Living here is not a long-term plan for me. I want to find a job elsewhere, but I lack the means. What should we do?"

Yun said, "I'm also considering it. Do you remember your brother-in-law, Fan Hui, who is now working as an accountant at the Jingjiang Salt Administration? Ten years ago, he borrowed ten taels of silver from you, but at the time, you didn't have enough silver, so I pawned my hairpin to make up for it. Do you remember?"

I said, "I forgot."

Yun said, "I heard that Jingjiang is not far from Xishan. Why don't you go and see?"

I followed Yun's suggestion.

At that time, the weather was relatively warm, wearing a padded robe and a short jacket, I still felt hot. This day was the sixteenth day of the first month of the year Xin-You (1801).

That night, I stayed at a lodge in Xishan and rented a blanket to sleep.

In the morning, I boarded a boat to Jiangyin, but encountered headwinds along the way, followed by a light rain. By the time we reached the mouth of the Jiangyin River at night, the spring chill penetrated to the bone. I bought some wine to keep warm, and as a result, my silver coins in my pocket were spent. After hesitating for a night, I decided to pawn off some silver by taking off my shirt to cross the river.

On the nineteenth day, the north wind intensified, and the snowfall grew heavier. Overcome with sorrow, I shed tears, regretting spending my silver on wine when I should have saved it for room and boat fees. Just as I felt desolate and cold, I suddenly saw an old man wearing grass shoes and a felt hat, carrying a yellow bag on his back. Upon entering the inn, the old man looked up at me, as if we had met before.

I asked, "Sir, are you from Taizhou, surnamed Cao?"

He replied, "Sir, yes, I am. If it weren't for you, Sir, I would have died long ago. Now that my daughter is safe and sound, I often remember your kindness in saving us. I never expected to meet you here today. Why is Sir lingering here?"

It turned out that when I was serving as a staff member in Taizhou, there was a family surnamed Cao, with humble origins. They had a very beautiful daughter who was already engaged to someone else. A powerful man tried to obtain his daughter through usurious means, leading to a dispute that reached the authorities. I intervened and ensured that his daughter still married the originally promised family. The Cao family then entered government service and expressed their gratitude by kowtowing, which is how we met.

I recounted my encounter with the snow and my journey to him.

The man named Cao said, "If the weather clears up tomorrow, I will accompany you on your way." He then bought wine to treat me warmly.

On the twentieth day, just as the morning bell tolled, I heard shouts at the riverbank urging people to board the ship. I hastily got up and asked Cao to accompany me on the boat. Cao said, "No need to hurry. It's best to board the ship after eating your fill." So, he paid for my lodging and meals, and then took me out to drink. Because I had been staying here for several days and was anxious to catch the boat, I couldn't eat much, and reluctantly managed to eat two sesame cakes. After boarding the boat, the cold wind on the river made me shiver.

Cao said, "I heard that a person from Jiangyin committed suicide on the Jingjiang River. His wife hired this boat to go there. So, we must wait for the person who hired the boat to arrive before we can set sail."

I was hungry and cold, enduring the chill, and waited until noon before the boat finally set sail. By the time we arrived in Jingjiang, it was already dusk.

Cao said, "Jingjiang has two salt administration offices. Are you looking for the one inside the city or outside?" I followed him unsteadily and said, "I really don't know whether it's inside or outside the city." Cao said, "In that case, let's stay for now and visit tomorrow."

Entering the inn, my shoes and socks were soaked with mud. After drying them by the fire, I hastily ate, feeling extremely tired, and fell asleep soundly. When I woke up, half of my socks had been burnt by the fire, and Cao paid for my lodging and meals again.

I went to the salt administration office in the city to visit my old friend Hu Ken Tang. With the recommendation of the officials there, I found work in the office, responsible for clerical work, which finally brought some stability to my body and mind.

In the following year, in the eighth month of the year Ren-Xu (1802), I received a letter from Yun, saying, "My illness is completely cured, but I feel uneasy relying on the hospitality of strangers. I also want to go to Jiangyin and take a look at the beautiful scenery of Pingshan."

So, I rented two houses by the river outside the Chunmen Gate in Jiangyin. I personally went to the Hua family's house in Xishan and brought Yun over. Mrs. Hua gave us a young servant named Ashuang to help with cooking and heating, and we agreed to live close to each other next year.

At that time, it was early February, and the weather was warm and sunny.

With the silver borrowed from Jingjiang, I prepared my belongings and went to visit my old friend Hu Ken Tang at the salt administration office in Hanjiang. With the recommendation of the supervisors there, I found work in the office, responsible for clerical work, which finally brought some stability to my body and mind.

In the second year, in the spring of the year Gui-Hai (1803), Yun's blood disease recurred. I thought of going to Jingjiang again to seek assistance.

Yun said, "It's better to seek help from relatives than from friends."

I said, "You're right. However, although friends are concerned, they are all idle at home now and can't help much."

Yun said, "Fortunately, the weather has warmed up. You may not encounter snow on the way. I hope you go quickly and come back quickly, without worrying about me. If you suffer any more health problems, my guilt will be even greater."

At that time, my salary had already been suspended. I pretended to hire a donkey to ease her mind, but in reality, I walked with dry cakes along the way, eating as I went. Heading southeast, crossing the river twice, walking eighty or ninety li, and looking around, there were no villages or smoke. By the time it was past midnight, only the yellow sand could be seen, and the stars twinkled. I found a local earth god shrine, about five feet high, surrounded by a short wall, with two pine trees planted around it. So, I bowed to the earth god, praying, "I am Shen from Suzhou, lost on my way to relatives and arrived here. I hope to stay in your shrine for one night and beg for the mercy and protection of the gods." Then I moved the small stone incense burner to the side and tried it with my body, only half of which could fit inside. I wore my hat backwards to cover my face, sat inside with half of my body exposed below the knees, closed my eyes, and listened quietly to the wilderness, only hearing the rustling of the wind. At this time, my feet were tired, my spirit was weary, and I fell asleep in a daze.

When I woke up, the eastern sky was already bright. Suddenly, I heard the sound of footsteps outside the short wall. I hurried out to see that it was the local farmers passing by on their way to the market. Asking about the route to Jingjiang, they replied, "Travel south for ten li, and you will reach Taixing County; cross the county and head southeast, ten li to a earthen mound, cross eight earthen mounds, and you will reach Jingjiang. The road is wide and spacious all the way." So, I returned to the earth god shrine, restored the incense burner to its original position, bowed to thank the gods, and continued on my way. After passing through Taixing, there were carts and vehicles along the way that I could hitch a ride with.

In the afternoon, I arrived in Jingjiang. I went to the salt administration office to leave my calling card, but after a long time, the gatekeeper said, "Master Fan is on official business and has gone to Changzhou." Seeing the expression on his face, it seemed that there was some excuse. I asked, "When will he be back?" He replied, "I don't know." I said, "Even if it takes a year, I will wait for him to return."

The gatekeeper understood my meaning and asked me privately, "Are you Master Fan's close relative?"

I said, "If I weren't a close relative, I wouldn't wait for him to return."

The gatekeeper said, "You just wait for a while."

Three days later, the gatekeeper told me that Fan Huilai had returned. In total, I borrowed twenty-five taels of silver this time.

I hired a donkey and hurried back. Yun's complexion was pale and she was crying uncontrollably. When she saw me return, she hurriedly said, "Do you know about what happened yesterday at noon, when Ashuang ran away with our belongings? We've been searching everywhere, but still haven't found him. Losing the property is one thing, but the main issue is that his mother entrusted it to me before she left. If he returns home today, with the Yangtze River blocking his way, it's really worrying. If his parents hide him and use this to deceive us, what should we do? Moreover, how can I face my sworn sister?"

I said, "Please don't be anxious. You're worrying too much. Deceiving us by hiding the child would be targeting wealthy people. My wife and I are just getting by, what could he possibly gain by deceiving us? Besides, we brought him to Yangzhou for half a year, provided him with clothes and food, never once scolded or beat him, and the neighbors all know. The truth is, the little slave has lost all conscience, taking advantage of our precarious situation to steal and run away. The slave girl gifted by the Hua family is not a good person, it's understandable that she has no face to see you. How can you say you have no face to see her? Now we should go to the county office to file a report and prevent any further trouble."

Yun's expression eased slightly after hearing my words. However, from then on, she often talked in her sleep, frequently calling out "Ashuang ran away" or "Han Yuan, why did you betray me." Her condition worsened day by day.

I wanted to seek medical treatment, but Yun stopped me, saying, "My illness initially stemmed from the sadness of my younger brother running away and my mother's passing. Then it was because of emotional turmoil, followed by anger and excitement; usually, I worry too much, hoping to be a good wife, but things never go as planned, leading to symptoms like dizziness and absent-mindedness. They say, 'when the disease is in the vitals, even the best doctor's hands are tied,' so please don't waste any more money. Looking back on the twenty-three years with you, I've been greatly loved and cared for by you, never abandoned despite my stubbornness and wilfulness. Knowing someone like you, having a husband like you, I have no regrets in this life.

"Recalling the past, with warmth of plain clothes and satisfaction of simple meals, living in harmony; the leisurely times spent in gardens and pavilions like Canglang Pavilion and Xiaoshuang Building were truly like immortals in the mortal world. How many lifetimes does it take to achieve immortality? What kind of people are we? We dare not aspire to immortality. Forcing it would offend the Creator's resentment and immediately attract the interference of demons. In short, it's because you are too kind-hearted, and I am destined to suffer in this life." Then, she sobbed and said, "Life is short, eventually ending in death. Being separated from you halfway through life, suddenly parting forever, unable to serve you for the rest of my life or witness our son Fengsen getting married, truly makes it hard for me to let go." With that, tears fell like beans.

I struggled to contain my grief and comforted her, saying, "You've been sick for eight years, with many days of weakness. Why are you suddenly speaking such heartbreaking words today?"

Yun said, "I've been dreaming for days that my parents came to pick me up in a boat. Whenever I close my eyes, I feel my body floating up and down, as if walking in the clouds and mist, probably because my soul has left and only my body remains, right?"

I said, "It's just a restless spirit. Take some tonics, rest quietly, and you'll naturally recover."

Yun continued to cry and said, "If I still had a glimmer of hope, I wouldn't scare you with these words. Now that I'm close to death, if I don't say it now, there won't be another chance. The reason you've faced your parents' anger, the hardships of wandering, it's all because of me. After I die, my parents' joy will naturally be restored, and you will be relieved of worries. My parents are getting old, and after I die, you should hurry back home. If you can't afford to bring my remains home, you can temporarily leave them in Yangzhou and bring me back to my hometown later. I hope you will marry another woman of good character to take care of your parents, raise our children, and I can rest in peace." With that, Yun's pain was unbearable, and she burst into tears.

I said, "If you really leave me behind in this life, I have no intention of remarrying. Besides, 'the waters of the ocean are hard to measure, except for Wushan, nothing is impossible.'"

Yun held my hand, trying hard to say something else, but only repeated "in the next life" intermittently. Suddenly, she struggled to breathe, unable to speak, staring straight ahead. No matter how much I called out to her, Yun couldn't speak anymore, tears streaming down her cheeks. Gradually, her breath weakened, tears dried up, her soul elusive, and she passed away!

It was the thirtieth day of the third month in the Jiayin year of the Jiaqing reign (1803).

At that moment, I faced the solitary lamp, with no relatives in sight, empty-handed, and my heart shattered into pieces. This sorrow is endless!

Thanks to my friend Hu Kentang's assistance of ten taels of silver, I organized all the belongings in the house, sold everything off, and personally prepared Yun's funeral. Alas! Yun, a weak woman, had the heart and mind of a man. After marrying into my family, I was busy with food and clothing every day, lacking in financial resources, yet Yun never minded. When I lived at home, we only enjoyed discussing literary matters.

As a result of continuous illness and despair, she left with resentment. Who caused such a thing? I've let down my good friends at home, how can I explain it all? I advise couples in the world, not only should they not hate each other, but they also shouldn't be overly attached. As the saying goes, "The love between husband and wife doesn't last forever." Take me as a lesson!

On the day of her return to the netherworld, it is said that the souls of the deceased will return home with the return of the spirit. Therefore, the arrangement of the room is the same as before, and the deceased's old clothes are placed on the bed, while the old shoes are placed under the bed, waiting for the return of the deceased's soul to observe. This is called "collecting sight."

A Taoist priest is invited to perform rituals, first collecting the soul of the deceased onto the bed, then sending it away, known as "receiving the divine." In the customs of the Hanjiang area, food and drink are placed in the deceased's former room, and then the family leaves the house, known as "avoiding the divine." Therefore, there have been incidents of theft in the house due to avoiding the divine.

During Yun's mourning period, the landlord, who used to live with us, moved out to avoid it. The neighbors advised me to also prepare food and leave. I agreed, intending to meet Yun's spirit when it returned. My fellow townsman Zhang Yumen advised me, saying, "Evil begets evil, it's better to believe it's there than to try!" I said, "It's precisely because I believe it's there that I'm not avoiding it and waiting here. It's because of this that such a thing might happen." Zhang Yumen said, "If you offend the divine at the time of the return, it will be detrimental to the living. Even if the lady's soul returns, it's already separated by life and death. What I'm worried about is that what you want to see won't have a tangible form to touch, and what you should avoid won't be avoidable."

At that time, I persisted in saying, "Life and death have their own fates. If you truly care about me, how can you accompany me?"

Zhang Yumen said, "I'll be guarding outside. If you notice anything unusual, just call out and I'll come in immediately."

So I lit a lamp and entered the room. The room was arranged as before, but Yun's figure was nowhere to be seen. I couldn't help but cry at the sight. Then I worried that tears would blur my vision and prevent me from seeing Yun's spirit, so I wiped my tears and tried to keep my eyes wide open, sitting on the bed waiting. As I touched her old clothes, still emitting her scent, my heart couldn't help but ache, and I fell into a daze.

But then I realized, why did I fall asleep so quickly while waiting for her spirit to return? I opened my eyes and looked around, only to see the two candles on the table flickering with a greenish light, the flames shrinking to the size of a bean; I instantly felt a chill run down my spine, trembling all over, rubbing my hands against my forehead, and carefully watching the candles. The flames of the two candles gradually rose, reaching over a foot high, almost burning the paper-covered ceiling above. By the light of the candles, I looked around, and the flames suddenly shrank back to their previous size. My heart was pounding like pounding rice, my legs trembling, wanting to call out to Zhang Yumen outside the door to come in and see, but thinking of Yun's fragile soul, afraid it would be driven away by the daylight, so I called out Yun's name softly and prayed. The room was silent, with nothing to be seen. Then, the flames brightened again, no longer flickering.

I went out and told Zhang Yumen everything I saw. He admired my courage so much, not knowing that I was just momentarily infatuated.

After Yun's death, thinking of the ancient saying "wife, plum, and crane" by Lin Hejing, I gave myself the name "Mei Yi." I buried Yun temporarily on Jinguishan outside the west gate of Yangzhou, locally known as Haojiabao Pagoda. I bought a burial site and buried her there according to her wishes.

I brought Yun's tablet back to my home in Suzhou, and my mother was also very sad. Qingjun and Fengsen returned, crying as they put on mourning clothes. My younger brother Qitang came in and said, "Father's anger has not subsided yet. It's best for you to stay in Yangzhou, wait until father returns home, and I will write to you asking you to come back."

So I bid farewell to my mother, parted with my children, and wept bitterly. Returning to Yangzhou, I sold paintings to make a living, so I could often shed tears and lament by Yun's grave. It was a solitary and desolate existence. Occasionally passing by the old house, I would cry with sadness. On the Double Ninth Festival, the grass and trees on the neighboring graves were all yellow, but the grass on Yun's grave was still green. The caretaker said, "This is a good grave site, so the energy is strong." I silently prayed, "The autumn wind is already cold, and I'm still wearing thin clothes. If you have a spirit, please bless me to find a job and get through the end of this year, waiting for news from my hometown."

Soon after, Mr. Zhang Yu'an, a retainer of the Jiangdu Mansion, was going back to Zhejiang to bury his relatives, and he asked me to take over his position for three months. Only then was I able to prepare warm clothing. I sealed the official seal, left the office, and Zhang Yumen invited me to stay at his house. Zhang Yumen had also lost his job and was struggling to make ends meet, so we agreed to help each other. I lent him all the remaining twenty taels of silver, telling him, "This was originally for the expenses of moving my late wife's remains to Suzhou. Once you have news from my hometown, you can repay me."

That year, I stayed at Zhang Yumen's house for the New Year. Morning and evening, I divined, but there was still no news from my hometown.

In the spring of the year of Jiazi (1804), I received a letter from Qingjun, informing me that my father had fallen ill. I planned to return to Suzhou immediately, but I was worried about rekindling his past anger. While hesitating and waiting, I received another letter from Qingjun, sorrowfully informing me that my father had passed away. I felt a sharp pain, unable to express it. With no time for anything else, I hurried back to Suzhou, kneeling in front of my father's spirit, bowing and crying until blood flowed.

Alas! My father toiled his whole life, traveling far and wide. He had a worthless son like me, who neither brought him joy nor cared for him when he was sick, unable to escape the crime of unfiliality!

My mother saw me crying and asked, "Why did you only come back today?"

I said, "It's thanks to Qingjun's granddaughter's letter that I returned."

My mother glanced at my sister-in-law and said no more. I stayed at the mourning hall until after the 49th day, with no one discussing family matters or consulting me on funeral arrangements. Ashamed of my lack of filial piety, I didn't dare to inquire.

One day, creditors suddenly came to collect debts from me. I came out to respond, saying, "It's only right to pursue debts that are owed. However, my father's body isn't even cold yet, and you come to demand debts during the funeral, isn't that too much?" One of the men whispered to me, "We were sent here by someone else. You should leave first. We'll demand payment from the one who sent us." I said, "I'll repay what I owe. You all can leave now." They agreed and left.

Then I called Qitang and lectured him, saying, "Although I am unworthy, I have not committed any evil deeds. If it is said that I have inherited something, I have never received a single penny. This time, coming back for the funeral was originally the duty of a son, not to compete with you for inheritance. A real man stands on his own feet. Since I came alone, I will leave alone!" With that, I turned and went back into the mourning hall, unable to stop my tears.

Afterwards, I bowed to bid farewell to my mother, then went to say goodbye to Qingjun. I planned to leave home and hide in the deep mountains, like the ancient immortal Chisongzi.

While Qingjun was trying to dissuade me, my friends Xia Nanxun (styled Dan'an) and Xia Fengtai (styled Yishan), two brothers, tracked me down and strongly advised me, saying, "The family has fallen to such a state, it's indeed easy to become angry. But even though your father has passed, your mother is still alive, your wife has died, and your son is not yet of age. Do you really feel at ease leaving like this?" I said, "Then what should I do?" Xia Dan'an said, "It's hard for you to live alone. Stay at my house for now. I heard that Shizhuang Hall has news of your leave. Why not wait for him to come back and see what arrangements he has for you?" I said, "It's not even 100 days since the funeral, and the elders are still at home. It might be inconvenient." Xia Yishan said, "My brother and I invited you here precisely because of our father's wishes. If you still think it's inconvenient, there's a temple to the west of my house. The abbot there is my good friend. You can stay there for now. How about that?" I agreed to his suggestion.

Qingjun said, "With the properties left by our grandfather, there is no less than three or four thousand taels of silver. Since father doesn't want a single penny, should you also leave your belongings behind? I'll go get them and deliver them directly to your residence in the temple." So, in addition to my luggage, I also received several items left by my father, such as books, inkstones, and pen holders.

The monks in the temple arranged for me to stay in the Dabeige. Dabeige faced north and south, with a Buddha statue facing east; a room was separated at the west end, with a month window facing directly the Buddhist altar. This room was originally used by those doing Buddhist ceremonies to eat vegetarian meals, so I placed my bed there.

Next to the door stood a statue of Guan Yu holding a knife, looking very majestic. There was a large gingko tree in the courtyard, so thick that three people couldn't wrap their arms around it. Its shade covered the entire Dabeige, and when it was quiet at night, the sound of the wind was like a roar. Xia Yishan often brought wine, food, and fruits to drink with me, saying, "You live alone here. Aren't you afraid late at night?" I said, "I have always been upright and honest in my life, with no evil thoughts. What is there to be afraid of?"

After living there for a while, heavy rain poured down for more than thirty days and nights. I worried that the gingko tree would be broken by the wind and rain, crushing the beams and collapsing the house. Fortunately, it was protected by the spirits and remained unscathed. However, countless houses outside collapsed; nearby fields were completely flooded. I painted with the monks every day, oblivious to the events outside the temple.

At the end of September, the weather cleared up. Xia Yishan's father, named Chunxiang, was going to do business in Chongming and took me with him to help with accounting. As a result, I received twenty taels of silver as payment. When we returned, it was just in time for my father's burial. Qitang asked Fengsen to tell me, "Uncle, because the funeral expenses were not enough, he wants you to contribute another twenty taels of silver." I was ready to give him all the silver, but Xia Yishan wouldn't allow it and only let me give him half. So I went with Qingjun to the cemetery first. After the burial, I returned to the Dabeige.

At the end of September, Xia Yishan had a piece of land in Yongtaisha, East Sea. He took me there to collect the rent for two months. After lingering there for two months, we returned to Suzhou in late winter, and I moved to his house, the Xuehong Grass Hall, to spend the New Year. Truly, he is like my own brother!

In July of the year of Yichou (1805), Shizhuang Hall finally returned to Suzhou from the capital.

Shizhuang's name was Yunyu, styled Zhiru, and Shizhuang was his nickname. We had been childhood friends. He was the top scholar in the Gengxu year of Qianlong (1790), later serving as the magistrate of Chongqing in Sichuan. During the White Lotus Rebellion, he fought in the army for three years, with outstanding achievements. Upon his return, we were overjoyed to meet again.

Soon after, on the Double Ninth Festival, he took his family to Chongqing, Sichuan, to take up his post, inviting me to accompany him. So I went to my ninth sister's husband, Lu Shangwu's house, to bid farewell to my mother. Because my father's old house had already belonged to someone else. My mother instructed me, saying, "Your younger brother is not enough to rely on. You need to work hard on this journey. The revival of the family's reputation relies entirely on you."

When Fengsen escorted me halfway, he suddenly burst into tears, so I urged him not to send me off any further and to return home early.

As the boat sailed out of Jingkou, Shizhuang coincidentally had an old friend from the past, a scholar named Wang Tifu, who worked at the Huaiyang Salt Office. He took a detour to visit him, and I went with him, allowing me to visit Yunniang's grave once again. After the boat returned, we traveled upstream along the Yangtze River, visiting scenic spots along the way. In Jingzhou, Hubei, we learned of Shizhuang's appointment as the Commissioner of Tongguan. He left me and his son Dunfu, as well as his family, to temporarily reside in Jingzhou. Shizhuang himself traveled lightly, passing through Chengdu, crossing the plank road, and heading to Tongguan to take up his post.

In the year of Bingyin (1806), in February, Shizhuang's family finally arrived by waterway and landed at Fancheng. The journey was long, the expenses were enormous, the vehicle was heavy, and there were many people, with horses dying and carriages breaking along the way, experiencing much hardship. After arriving at Tongguan for only three months, Shizhuang was promoted to the position of Prosecutor of Mountain Left. Since his family could not accompany him due to his clean and upright nature, they temporarily stayed at the Shuyuan in Tongguan.

At the end of October, Shizhuang received the salary for his new position as Prosecutor of Mountain Left and sent someone to fetch his family. Among them was a letter from Qingjun's daughter for me, informing me with shock that my son Fengsen had passed away in April. Recalling the scene where he suddenly burst into tears on our way, it turned out that it was a farewell between father and son!

Alas! Yun had only this one son, and I couldn't continue her lineage!

Upon hearing the news, Shizhuang sighed deeply for me and gave me a concubine, allowing me to re-enter the realm of tenderness. From then on, the world was tumultuous, and I didn't know when I would finally wake up!

VOLUME FOUR: TRAVELS AND ADVENTURES

In my thirty years of serving as a secretary in various places, there were only a few places I hadn't visited, such as Sichuan, Guizhou, and Yunnan. Unfortunately, every time I traveled, it was in a hurry, following others everywhere. The joy that mountains and rivers bring to people is like a fleeting cloud, only to be superficially appreciated without the opportunity to delve deep into their beauty.

In all things, I prefer to have my own opinions and disdain to follow others in praising or criticizing. Even when it comes to poetry and painting, I always keep in mind the principle of "treasuring what others discard, and discarding what others treasure." Therefore, the essence of traveling to famous places lies in finding ones that resonate with my heart, where there is true beauty that may not necessarily be recognized by others. Let me record the experiences of my life so far.

When I was fifteen years old, my father, Gong Jiafu, served in the office of Zhao Ming, the magistrate of Shanyin. There was a Mr. Zhao Shengzhai, renowned for his scholarship in Hangzhou, who was hired by Magistrate Zhao to tutor his children. My father also arranged for me to study under him.

During leisure breaks from studying, I had the opportunity to visit Mount Hou. Mount Hou was more than ten miles from Shanyin County and had no road accessible by land. There was a stone cave at the foot of the mountain, with a slab of stone above it that seemed almost about to fall, and we rowed a boat underneath it to enter. Inside, it was suddenly spacious, with cliffs on all sides, known locally as the "Water Garden." Five stone pavilions were built by the water, and on the opposite cliff was inscribed the words "Fish Watching Pavilion." The depth of the water was unfathomable, and it was said that a giant fish lurked within. I cast some bait into the water and saw fish less than a foot long come to feed. Behind the stone pavilions, there was a path leading to the dry garden, where scattered fist-sized rocks stood, some as broad as a palm, and others with large stones placed on top of flat pillar stones, with traces of chiseling still visible, but there was nothing remarkable about them.

After finishing our visit, we feasted and drank in the Water Pavilion. I ordered the attendants to set off firecrackers, and with a loud bang, the mountains echoed as if thunder had struck. Thus began my youthful wanderings. Unfortunately, I never had the opportunity to visit the Orchid Pavilion or the Tomb of Yu, which remain regrets to this day.

In my second year in Shanyin, my teacher set up a school at home because his elderly parents could not travel far. I followed him to Hangzhou, where I had the opportunity to enjoy the beauty of West Lake.

Among the scenic spots of West Lake, Longjing (Dragon Well) was the most exquisite in layout and structure, followed by Tianyuan (Heavenly Garden). As for the beauty of the mountains and rocks, there was the Feilai Peak in front of Lingyin Temple, which seemed to have flown from India, and the ancient cave rocks of Chenghuang Mountain. Among the springs, there was Yuquan (Jade Spring), because of its clear water and abundant fish, which had a lively charm. Perhaps the least impressive at first glance was the Agate Temple on Gelingshan (Ge Ridge).

Other places such as Huxin Pavilion and Liuyi Spring each had their own charm, which cannot be described in detail. However, they all seemed to be unable to escape the artificial beauty, unlike the tranquility and natural elegance of Xiaojing Pavilion.

Su Xiaoxiao's tomb is located next to Xiling Bridge. Local people say that initially, it was just a half-hill of yellow soil. In the year of Gengzi during the Qianlong reign, the emperor visited here during his southern tour and inquired about this tomb. By the spring of the Jiachen year, when the emperor visited again, Su Xiaoxiao's tomb had been built with stones. The tomb is octagonal, with a stele inscribed with the large characters "Tomb of Su Xiaoxiao in Qiantang." Since then, poets and scholars who longed for ancient times no longer need to search everywhere. Since ancient times, there have been countless loyal and steadfast people who have been buried and forgotten. Even for those whose fame did not last long and soon faded into obscurity, there were many. Su Xiaoxiao was just a courtesan, but her name and deeds have been known to everyone from the Southern Qi dynasty to the present day. This is probably because the spirits of heaven and earth favored this place and added some embellishments to its scenery.

Not far north of the bridge, there is a Chongwen Academy, where I once visited with my classmate Zhao Ji. It happened to be the height of summer when we rose very early, passed through Qiantang Gate, went through Zhaoqing Temple, and walked onto the Broken Bridge, where we sat on the stone railing. We could see the sunrise about to rise, the morning glow reflecting through the willows, all displaying their beauty; the lotus flowers in the lake emitted a fragrance, and the gentle breeze blew, refreshing the mind and body.

We walked to the academy, but the exam questions had not yet been announced. In the afternoon, after submitting our papers, Zhao Ji and I relaxed in Ziyun Cave. The cave could accommodate dozens of people, with sunlight filtering through the stone holes, and some people had set up low tables and stools to sell wine. Zhao Ji and I enjoyed some drinks and tasted deer jerky in the cave, feeling wonderfully refreshed. We also ate some fresh water chestnuts and lotus roots until we were slightly intoxicated before leaving the cave.

Zhao Ji said, "There is a Sunrise Terrace on the mountain, which is quite elevated. Why don't we go and explore?" I was also interested, so we bravely climbed to the mountaintop. From there, we could see West Lake like a mirror, Hangzhou City like a tiny bead, and the Qiantang River like a ribbon, stretching for hundreds of miles. This was the first time in my life that I had seen such a magnificent sight.

We sat on the Sunrise Terrace for a long time, and as the sun was setting, we descended the mountain. The evening bell of the Nanping Mountain Buddha Temple also rang. We did not have time to visit places like Taoguang and Yunqi, and other attractions such as the plum blossoms of Hongmen Bureau and the iron trees of Aunt Temple were just mentioned in passing. I thought the Ziyun Cave would be worth seeing, but when we arrived, we found that the entrance could only accommodate one finger, with a trickle of water flowing through it. It was said that there were hidden wonders inside, but unfortunately, we could not pry open the door to enter.

On Qingming Festival, my teacher went to the mountains to pay respects to his ancestors and invited me to accompany him.

The tomb is in Dongyue, where bamboo grows abundantly. The tombkeeper dug up some tender shoots that had not yet emerged from the ground, resembling pears but sharper, and cooked them into a soup for guests. I liked it very much and ate two bowls. My teacher said, "Hmm! Although these bamboo shoots taste delicious, they consume blood and energy, so it's best to eat more meat to counteract their effects." I had never been fond of meat, and my appetite decreased after eating too many shoots. On the way back, I felt restless, and my lips almost cracked.

Passing by Shiwu Cave, I found nothing worth seeing. Water Music Cave was covered with vines on the cliff, and entering it felt like entering a fighting arena; the spring water flowed swiftly with a tinkling sound, and the water pool was only three feet wide and more than five inches deep, neither overflowing nor drying up. I bent down to drink a few mouthfuls of spring water, and the restlessness in my heart disappeared instantly.

Outside Shiwu Cave, there were two small pavilions where one could hear the sound of the spring water. Monks invited us to see the Millennium Jar; it was located in the Xiangji kitchen, extremely large in size, and bamboo pipes led spring water into the jar, allowing it to overflow. Over time, a layer of moss more than a foot thick formed inside the jar, which never froze in winter and therefore remained undamaged.

In the autumn of the year Xinchou, my father fell ill with malaria and returned home. He felt cold but asked for fire, hot but asked for ice. I advised him, but he didn't listen and eventually developed typhoid fever, and his condition worsened day by day. I nursed my father, bringing him soup and medicine, and stayed awake day and night for almost a month.

At this time, my wife Yunniang also fell seriously ill and lay weakly in bed. My state of mind was indescribable. My father called me to his bedside and said, "I'm afraid my illness won't be cured. Relying on a few books is not a way to make a living. I entrusted you to my sworn brother, Jiang Sizhai. When the time comes, you can take over my business." The next day, Jiang Sizhai came to my house, and I obediently bowed to him as my teacher in front of my father's sickbed.

Soon after, with the treatment of the famous physician Mr. Xu Guanlian, my father's illness gradually improved. Yunniang also received assistance from Mr. Xu Guanlian and was able to get out of bed. From then on, I began to learn how to make a living by serving as a secretary. This was not a pleasant thing, so why record it?

Because this was the beginning of my wandering after abandoning books, so I recorded it.

Mr. Jiang Sizhai's name was Xiang. That winter, I followed him to study in Fengxian Government Office. There was a classmate studying with me, whose surname was Gu, named Jinjian, with the courtesy name Honggan and the sobriquet Zixia, also from Suzhou. He was generous and resolute, straightforward and uncompromising. He was a year older than me, so I called him elder brother. He, in turn, called me younger brother. We developed a close friendship, and he was the first true friend I had in my life. Unfortunately, he passed away at the age of twenty-two. From then on, I was alone, with very few friends. I am already forty-six years old this year, and in the vast ocean of life, will I ever meet another friend like Zixia?

Recalling my friendship with Zixia, we both harbored lofty ideals and often thought of retiring to the mountains and forests. During the Double Ninth Festival, Zixia and I were both in Suzhou. A senior named Wang Xiaoxia invited my father to watch a female performer at our house. I didn't like the noise, so I made an appointment with Zixia to climb Hanshan and visit places for future seclusion. Yunniang prepared a box of wine and food for us.

The next day, just before dawn, Zixia came to my door. So I brought the wine utensils and went out from Xumen, eating separately in a noodle shop. We crossed the Xujia River and walked to Zaoshi Bridge in Hengtang Town, where we hired a small boat. When we arrived at Hanshan, it was not yet noon. The boatman was quite honest and kind, so we let him buy rice to cook for us. The two of us landed and climbed the mountain, first arriving at Zhongfeng Temple. Zhongfeng Temple is located on the south side of Zhixing Mountain, hidden in deep forests, and the mountain gate is silent and deserted. As it was remote and the monks were idle, the mountain monks were not very willing to receive us since our purpose was not there.

We returned to the boat after descending the mountain, and the rice was already cooked. After eating, the boatman carried the wine utensils to follow us, instructing his son to guard the small boat. We walked from Hanshan to the White Cloud Hermitage of Gaoyi Garden. The pavilion was close to the cliff, with a square pool carved below, surrounded by artificial mountains and bushes; looking down, we could see a pool of autumn water, the passion fruit vines on the cliff, and the moss growing on the wall. We sat below the pavilion, hearing only the rustling of falling leaves, quiet and devoid of human presence.

Outside the gate, there was a pavilion, and we instructed the boatman to sit inside and wait. The two of us squeezed through a gap in the rocks, which led to the "One-Line Sky"; ascending the steps, we spiraled up until we reached the mountaintop, which was the "Above White Clouds." At the mountaintop, there was a ruined nunnery, with only a dilapidated tower remaining, which we could climb up to for a distant view. After resting for a moment, we descended the mountain with assistance.

The boatman said, "You forgot to bring wine utensils for your climb."

Zixia replied, "We're here to explore and find a place for seclusion, not specifically for climbing."

The boatman suggested, "About two or three miles south of here is Shangsha Village, which has many households and some empty land; my cousin with the surname Fan lives in this village. Why not go and take a look?"

I exclaimed, "That's where Mr. Xu Sizhai secluded himself during the Ming Dynasty. I heard the garden there is extremely elegant, and I haven't been there yet." So the boatman led us there.

The village was situated between two mountains, with the garden built against the mountainside. Instead of using mountain stones, the old trees were twisted and lush, with simple pavilions and windows, bamboo fences, and thatched cottages, truly a place suitable for a hermit. In the garden was a Soapberry Pavilion, with trees so thick that two people would need to hug them together. Among all the garden pavilions I've seen, this one was the best.

To the left of the garden was a mountain called "Chicken Cage Mountain," with a steep peak and a large rock on top, similar to the Rui Shi Ancient Cave in Hangzhou, but not as exquisite. Next to it was a green stone that looked like a bed; Zixia lay down on it and said, "This place offers a view of the mountain peaks and ridges above, overlooking the beauty of the garden below. It's both open and serene, perfect for enjoying a drink." So he persuaded the boatman to join us for some wine, and we sang and laughed heartily, feeling completely at ease.

The locals, thinking we had come to look at feng shui, enthusiastically pointed out places with good feng shui. Zixia remarked, "We only seek a place that suits our hearts and minds, regardless of its feng shui." Who would have thought that this statement would become a prophecy!

We drank until the wine was gone, then picked wildflowers to adorn our hair. As we sailed back home, the sun was about to set. We returned home around midnight, but the guests were still there.

Yunniang privately told me, "Among the female performers, there's one named Lan Guan, who has a dignified appearance."

I pretended to receive a message from my mother and called her into the bedroom, carefully examining her hand. Indeed, her cheeks were plump and her skin fair. I said to Yunniang, "She's truly beautiful, but her name doesn't seem to match her."

Yunniang said, "Plumpness is a sign of good fortune."

I retorted, "Then where was Yang Yuhuan's good fortune during the chaos at Ma Wei Slope?"

Yunniang made up an excuse to send Lan Guan away, then asked me, "Did you get drunk again today?"

I detailed what I had seen during our excursion, and Yunniang was amazed.

In the spring of the year Gui Mao, I accompanied Mr. Zhao Sizhai to the Weiyang Prefectural Office, where I saw Jinshan and Jiaoshan for the second time. Jinshan was best viewed from afar, while Jiaoshan was best appreciated up close. Unfortunately, although I traveled between the two mountains, I did not climb to enjoy the distant view. Crossing the river northward, I saw Wang Yuyang's poem "The city walls of Liyang are Yangzhou" vividly displayed before my eyes.

Pingshantang was three or four miles from the city of Yangzhou, and it was another eight or nine miles from there. Although the scenery along the way was all man-made, the ingenious ideas and natural embellishments were such that even Lan Yuan's Jade Pools and Qiong Lou's Jade Pavilions probably couldn't surpass it. What was most remarkable was that more than ten garden pavilions merged into one harmonious entity, seamlessly connected to the mountains above. The most difficult part was entering the scenic area outside the city and walking about a mile, which was adjacent to the city wall.

Generally, cities are built between vast mountains to evoke a sense of artistic conception; however, if a garden were located in such a place, it would appear awkward. But Pingshantang, with its pavilions, towers, walls, rocks, bamboo groves, and trees, all half-hidden and half-revealed, did not seem abrupt to visitors. Such planning would be difficult to execute without a person of great insight.

At the end of the city, there was Hongyuan Garden. Turning north, there was a stone bridge called "Hong Bridge." It's unclear whether the garden was named after the bridge or vice versa. Crossing the bridge, we reached "Changdi Spring Willows"; the placement of these scenes outside the city rather than at its foot made the layout even more ingenious. From there, we turned westward and built a mound into a hill, where a temple named "Xiao Jinshan" was erected; overall, the layout felt compact and well-organized, not superficial. I heard that this place was originally sandy soil, and despite several attempts, it couldn't be built successfully; later, a number of wooden planks were used, stacked with soil layers, costing tens of thousands of taels of silver to complete. Only a wealthy merchant could afford such extravagance.

After passing Xiao Jinshan, we reached Shenggailou, where people gather annually to watch dragon boat races. The river was relatively wide here, with a lotus flower bridge spanning from north to south. The bridge led to five pavilions on its surface, known as the "Four Plates and One Warm Pot" by the people of Yangzhou, which seemed like a forced attempt at symbolism. To the south of the bridge was Lianxin Temple, where a white pagoda of Lamaism stood tall, its golden spire and hanging pearls shining against the sky; the temple's corners and red walls were hidden among the green pines and cypresses, with the sound of bells and chimes occasionally heard. This was a splendid scene not found in any other garden pavilion.

After crossing the lotus flower bridge, one could see a three-story high tower with painted eaves, colorful and magnificent, with a man-made hill made of Taihu rocks piled up around it; white jade railings surrounded it on all sides. This place was called "Wuyun Duo Chu," like the central structure in a composition. Beyond this, there was "Shugang Chaohu," a flat and unremarkable hill that was often embellished. As we approached the foot of the mountain, the river gradually narrowed, and the banks were piled with soil and planted with bamboo and other trees. After turning four or five bends in the seemingly endless river, the Wan Songlin of Pingshan finally appeared before us.

The three words "Pingshan Tang" were written by Ouyang Xiu.

The so-called "Fifth Spring of Huaidong" was actually just a well inside a fake mountain cave, nothing more than a well with the same taste as Tianquan water. As for the six-hole iron well railings in the He Ting, they were purely decorative, as the well water was undrinkable. The Jiufeng Garden was located in a secluded area near the south gate, unique and charming; I thought it was the best among the many gardens. I didn't visit Kangshan Caotang, so I'm not sure about it.

These scenes I've described only briefly; their ingenious construction and exquisite craftsmanship cannot be fully conveyed. In general, it's best to see them as a beautiful woman in makeup rather than a Xi Shi on Huan Sha River. I happened to witness the emperor's southern inspection during its peak, with various newly built projects completed, and local governments respectfully advancing preparations for his arrival, allowing me to enjoy this grand event, which was a rare opportunity in life.

In the spring of the year Jia Chen, I accompanied my father to the prefectural office of Wang Ming in Haining, where I worked with colleagues such as Shan Yin Zhang Pinjiang, Wu Lin Zhang Yingmu, and Tiao Xi Gu Aiquan on the affairs of the Nandou Weir Palace, and I saw the emperor's face for the second time.

One day, as evening approached, I suddenly felt the urge to go home. At that time, there was a small, fast boat for official business, with double oars and double paddles. I boarded the boat and swiftly rowed across Taihu Lake. In an instant, I arrived at Wumen Bridge. Even if I were flying in the sky on a crane, it wouldn't have been as invigorating as this trip. When I arrived home, dinner was not yet ready.

My hometown has always admired splendor, and at such times, the striving for excellence surpasses that of the past. With lanterns and decorations dazzling the eyes, music and singing incessant, it felt overwhelmingly noisy. The "painted beams and carved rafters," "pearl curtains and embroidered curtains," "jade railings" and "brocade barriers" mentioned by ancient people probably couldn't compare to this moment. I was pulled in all directions by friends, helping them with flower arrangements and decorations, and in my spare time, I called friends to drink and sing, thoroughly enjoying the festivities.

In the exuberance of youth, there is no fatigue. If one were born in a prosperous era but lived in a remote village, how could they experience such travels and sights?

  That year, due to certain circumstances, Prefect He Ming was dismissed from his position, and my father was transferred to the prefectural office of Wang Ming in Haining.

  In Jiaxing, there was a man named Liu Huijie, who ate vegetarian food and believed in Buddhism. He came to visit my father. His house was next to Yan Yu Lou, with a loft facing the river called "Shuiyueju," where he recited Buddhist scriptures, a place as clean as a monk's quarters. Yan Yu Lou was located in the middle of Jing Lake, surrounded by green willows on all sides, though there were few bamboo trees. There was also a platform for distant viewing, where fishing boats dotted the surface like stars, and a thin mist hung over the water, making it seem more suitable for viewing on a moonlit night. The vegetarian meals prepared by the monks were delicious.

  Upon arriving at the Mu Mansion in Haining, I worked alongside my colleagues Bai Men Shi Xinyue and Shan Yin Yu Wuqiao. Xinyue had a son named Zhu Heng, who was serene in temperament, spoke little, and treated others with gentlemanly manners. We became close friends, the second most intimate friend I've had in my life. It's a pity that our encounters were fleeting.

  We toured the Chen Family's Peaceful Garden, which covered an area of 100 mu (about 6.7 hectares), with towering buildings, pavilions, and winding corridors. Among them was a large pond with six curved bridges, beautifully shaped. Ivy covered the rocks, concealing every chisel mark, while ancient trees, with their towering presence, created an atmosphere akin to being deep in the mountains. This was a model of artificial construction approaching the beauty of nature. Among all the artificial rockeries and pavilions I've visited on the plains, the Peaceful Garden was the best.

  We also held banquets and entertained guests in the Guihua Tower within the garden. Despite the aroma of numerous dishes, the fragrance of the flowers covered them all, except for the unchanged scent of ginger sauce. Ginger and cassia, as they age, become spicier; this served as a metaphor for the unwavering loyalty of faithful ministers, a comparison that holds true.

  Exiting the south gate of Haining, we encountered the sea. The tide rose twice a day, resembling a silver dike reaching thousands of feet high, breaking through the sea. Boats facing the tide would reverse their oars as the tide approached, placing a wooden sign resembling a long-handled broadsword at the bow. When the sign was pressed, the tide would part, allowing the boat to enter. After a brief pause, it would float out again. At this point, the boat would turn its bow and follow the tide, covering a hundred li (about 50 kilometers) in an instant.

On the sea dike stood a tower courtyard. On Mid-Autumn night, I once watched the tide here with my father. About thirty li to the east along the sea dike was a mountain called Jian Mountain, with a peak jutting out as if plunging into the sea. At the summit was a pavilion with the words "Vast Sea and Sky" inscribed on the plaque. Looking out from the tower, the view was boundless, with nothing but raging waves meeting the sky.

When I was twenty-five years old, I accepted an appointment from the governor of Huizhou, Ke Ming, and traveled by boat from Wulin, passing through the Fuchun Mountains to visit the Ziling Fishing Platform. The fishing platform, located halfway up the mountain, rose more than ten zhang (about 30 meters) above the water's surface. Was the water level during the Han Dynasty really level with this peak? On a clear night, we stopped the boat at Jiekou, next to the inspection office. As Su Shi's "After the Red Cliff" poem says, "The mountains are high, the moon is small, and the water falls to reveal the rocks." This scene was right before my eyes. Unfortunately, I only saw the foothills of Huangshan; it was regrettable that I did not ascend to admire the scenery.

The city of Jixi is nestled among mountains. Although it is a small town, the people are simple and sincere. Near the city is a mountain called Shijing Mountain, with a winding path that twists and turns for more than a mile, with cliffs and rushing streams, dripping with moisture. As we ascended the mountain, we could see a square stone pavilion surrounded by steep cliffs on all sides. The left side of the pavilion was as smooth as if it had been carved by a knife, shining with a blue light like a screen, casting clear shadows of people. Legend has it that it can reflect one's past life. When Huang Chao passed through here, he reflected an image of a monkey, which he set on fire and destroyed, hence it could no longer reflect past lives.

Ten li away from the city, there is a place called "Fire Cloud Cave." The rocks there are interwoven with intricate patterns, rugged and steep, resembling the brushstrokes of a painter on Huangshan Mountain, but the overall appearance is disorderly and lacks order. The stones inside the cave are all deep red in color, and there is a temple nearby, very quiet. Salt merchant Cheng Xugu once invited me to visit and host a feast here. Among the dishes was a kind of meat bun that caught the attention of a novice monk, so I gave him four. When we left, I gave him two rounds of foreign silver as a thank you, but the monk refused to accept it, saying there was no place nearby to exchange it. Finally, the crowd pooled together six hundred copper coins for him, which he reluctantly accepted. The next day, I invited my companions to bring wine utensils and go again. The old monk warned, "The novice had diarrhea after eating something last time, so please don't give him any this time." From this, it can be seen that a stomach accustomed to wild vegetables such as goosefoot finds it difficult to digest meat. It's truly sigh-inducing.

I said to my companions, "To become a monk, one must live in such remote places, never seeing or hearing anything unusual in one's lifetime. Perhaps only then can one cultivate true tranquility. If one were to live in a place like my hometown of Tiger Hill, where every evening is filled with enchanting beauties, where one's ears are filled with the sounds of music, and where one's nose is filled with the aroma of fine wine and delicacies, how could one's body be like withered wood and one's heart like dead ashes?"

Thirty li from the city, there is a place called Renli, where a grand flower and fruit festival is being held. The festival is held every twelve years, and each participant competes with potted flowers they have planted. When I was in Jixi, I happened to encounter this event. Eager to attend, I was troubled by the lack of sedan chairs and horses. So, I instructed someone to cut bamboo into poles, tied them to chairs as poles, and hired people to carry them on their shoulders. Only my colleague Xu Ceting accompanied me, and everyone we met along the way was surprised and laughed.

Upon arriving at Renli, there was a temple, but I didn't know what deity it worshipped. In the spacious front yard of the temple, there was a towering stage, elaborately painted with beams and pillars, extremely majestic. However, upon closer inspection, it was nothing more than paper-mâché and paint. Suddenly, the sound of gongs came from afar. Four people carried a pair of candles, as large as a broken beam; eight people carried a pig, as fat as a bull. It turned out that everyone had raised the pig for twelve years before slaughtering it as an offering to the deity.

Ceting laughed and said, "Pigs may be long-lived, but gods also have sharp teeth. If I were a god, how could I enjoy it?"

I said, "From this, we can also see the ignorance and piety of the people here."

Entering the temple, the potted plants arranged in the hall, corridors, and courtyards were not pruned or tied, but rather left with gnarled and peculiar shapes, mostly Huangshan pines. Then, the drama began, and the crowd surged in like a tide. Ceting and I had to withdraw and leave.

Less than two years later, I had a falling-out with my colleagues and left abruptly, returning to Suzhou from Jixi.

After my travels in Jixi, I witnessed various despicable acts in the bustling scenes, which were unbearable to see. Therefore, I turned to scholarship and commerce. I had an uncle named Yuan Wanjia, who ran a liquor business in Panxi's Xianren Pond. I partnered with Shi Xingeng to provide capital. Yuan Wanjia's liquor was originally sold by sea, but within a year, the Taiwan Lin Shuangwen rebellion interrupted the sea route, causing goods to pile up and losses to accrue. With no other choice, we returned to our old business and worked as clerks in Jiangbei for four years, without any enjoyable travels to record.

Until I lived in the Xiao Shuang Pavilion, where Yun Niang and I were engaged in fireworks and immortality, my cousin-in-law Xu Xiufeng returned from eastern Guangdong and saw me living leisurely at home. He sighed and said, "Depending on dew to cook rice and relying on writing for a living is not a long-term solution. Why don't you come with me to explore Lingnan? Surely you'll gain more than just meager profits." Yun also persuaded me, saying, "While your parents are still healthy, and you are in your prime, instead of daily worries about livelihood and pleasure-seeking, why not make a decisive move?"

So, I discussed with my friends and raised the capital. Yun also purchased some textiles and embroideries, as well as Suzhou wine and drunken crabs, items that were not available in Lingnan. Then, I informed my parents, and in the tenth month of the lunar calendar, during the minor sunny period, Xu Xiufeng and I departed from Dongba and headed to Lingnan via Wuhu Port.

Traveling the Yangtze River for the first time, I was in extremely high spirits. Every night after docking, we would have a small drink at the bow of the ship.

Once, we saw fishermen using nets that were less than three feet long but had mesh sizes of four inches. They were fixed with iron hoops at the four corners, seemingly designed for easy sinking into the water.

I laughed and said, "Although the sages say 'countless are the nets not used,' how can nets so large in mesh and small in size expect to catch anything?"

Xiufeng said, "These are specifically designed nets for catching freshwater eels."

We saw these nets being tethered with long ropes, rising and falling on the water's surface as if testing for fish. After a while, they hurriedly pulled them out of the water, and there were already freshwater eels stuck tightly in the mesh. At that moment, I sighed and said, "From this, it can be seen that my previous opinion was just my own, unable to grasp the mysteries within."

One day, while traveling by boat, we saw a peak in the middle of the river, towering and surrounded by nothing. Xiufeng said, "That's Xiaogu Mountain." In the frosty forest on Xiaogu Mountain, temples and pavilions were scattered about haphazardly. Unfortunately, we passed by in our boat, unable to stop and explore.

Upon reaching Tengwang Pavilion, it felt as if our Suzhou Prefectural School's Zunjing Pavilion had been moved to the bustling docks of Xumen. Wang Zian's preface seemed unbelievable. So, we changed to a high-tailed boat called "Sanbanzi" and traveled directly to Nan'an from Gan Guan, only stopping to disembark. It happened to be my thirtieth birthday, and Xiufeng prepared longevity noodles to celebrate for me.

The next day, as we passed through the Dayu Mountains, we saw a pavilion on the mountaintop with the words "Looking Up, The Sun Is Near," describing the height of the mountain. The mountain was split in two, with steep cliffs on both sides, and the road in the middle resembled a stone alley. At the intersection, two stone steles were erected, one with the words "Retreat in the Face of Swift Currents" and the other with the words "Satisfied, Don't Proceed Further." There was also a General Mei Shrine at the mountain peak, but it was unclear which dynasty it belonged to. The legendary plum blossoms on the mountain were nowhere to be seen. Could it be that the mountain was named Meiling after General Mei? The potted plum I brought along arrived at Meiling in late December, with the flowers already withered and the leaves turning yellow.

After crossing the Dayu Mountains and leaving the mountain

pass, the scenery immediately felt distinctly different from that of Wuyue. There was a mountain to the west with a delicate stone cave on top, but I've forgotten its name. The sedan bearers said, "There's a immortal's bed in the stone cave." Unfortunately, we hurried past and couldn't stop to visit.

After arriving in Nanxiong, we hired an old dragon boat and continued our journey. In Foshan Town, we saw many households placing potted flowers on their walls. The leaves resembled holly, and the flowers resembled peonies, coming in three colors: crimson, pink, and pale pink. These were camellia flowers.

It wasn't until the fifteenth day of the twelfth lunar month that we arrived in the provincial capital of Guangdong and settled in within the Jinghai Gate. We rented a three-room street-facing house from a family surnamed Wang. Xiu Feng's goods were all sold to officials and merchants, and I followed suit in entertaining guests. Soon, people came to collect the goods for their arranged marriages, and the demand was constant. In less than ten days, all the goods I brought had been sold.

On New Year's Eve, the mosquito buzz was still thunderous. During the Spring Festival, there were people dressed in padded robes and others in gauze jackets. Not only was the climate vastly different from that of Wu, but even the local residents, with the same facial features, exhibited different expressions and temperaments.

On the sixteenth day of the twelfth lunar month, three fellow provincials from government offices invited me to watch river-viewing and courtesans. The locals called it "Water Enclosure," and the courtesans were referred to as "Old Jus." So, we left the Jinghai Gate and went down to a small boat resembling a uniformly halved egg with a canopy on top, reaching Sha Men first.

The courtesan boat was called a "flower boat," with the bow of each boat arranged in pairs, leaving a passage in the middle for small boats to pass through. Each group of courtesans had about ten to twenty boats tied together with crossbeams to withstand the sea breeze. Between two boats, wooden stakes were nailed, wrapped in rattan rings, rising and falling with the tide. The madam was called the "hairdressing mother," with her hair held up by a silver wire hairpin, about four inches high, with a hollow middle and hair coiled around it, adorned with a flower at the temple. She wore a dark blue short jacket, green trousers, with the trouser legs dragging on her feet. A towel was tied around her waist, in red or green, and she wore embroidered butterfly shoes on bare feet, the size resembling those worn by actresses in a theater.

 Boarding her boat, she greeted us with a bow and a smile, drawing back the curtain to invite guests into the cabin. Inside the cabin were chairs and stools on both sides, with a large bed in the middle, and a door leading to the stern of the boat. When the madam shouted "We have guests," the sound of footsteps came rushing in, with the courtesans having different hairstyles, some with braids, some with coiled hair, faces painted as white as walls, and lips as red as pomegranate flowers. They wore either red jackets and green trousers or green jackets and red trousers, some wearing short socks with embroidered butterfly shoes, others wearing silver anklets on bare feet. Some squatted on the bed, some leaned against the door, eyes sparkling, but not saying a word.

 I turned to Xiu Feng and asked, "What does this mean?" Xiu Feng said, "You need to gesture to indicate your choice, and then they will approach you." So, I tentatively chose one person, and indeed, she came forward with a smile, taking out a betel nut from her sleeve as a gesture of respect. I put the betel nut in my mouth and chewed it, but it was so bitter that I couldn't bear it and hurriedly spit it out. Wiping my mouth with a tissue, what I spat out was as red as blood, causing everyone on the boat to burst into laughter.

 We also visited the military factory, where the courtesans were dressed similarly, but they were all proficient in playing the pipa. When talking to them, their answers were all "Huh?" "Huh?" What does this mean? I said to my friends, "As the saying goes, 'Youth doesn't enter Guang,' because the courtesans here are captivating. If they were dressed and spoke coarsely, who would be interested?"

 A friend said, "The courtesans of the Chao gang are like fairies, and you should visit them." So, we went to the Chao gang courtesan boat, where the scene was similar to Sha Men. There was a famous madam named Su Niang, whose dressing resembled a woman playing flower drums. The courtesans under her all wore long collars with necklaces, their hair arranged to reach their eyebrows in the front and shoulders at the back, with a maid-like bun in the middle. They wore skirts with bound feet, while Tianzu wore short socks. They also wore butterfly shoes, with the trousers dragging on the ground. Their language was understandable. However, I still didn't like their peculiar dressing, and my interest waned.

 Xiu Feng said, "Opposite Jinghai Gate, there are courtesans from the Yang gang, all dressed in Wu style. If you go there, you will surely find someone to your liking." A friend said, "The so-called Yang gang only has one madam, known as Widow Shao, accompanied by a daughter-in-law named Daguniang, who indeed came from Yangzhou. The rest are courtesans from Hubei and Jiangxi."

So, we went to the Yang gang courtesan boat. The boats were arranged in pairs, with only about a dozen small boats. The courtesans there all had cloud-like hair, thin powder on their faces, wide-sleeved long skirts, and clear speech. The madam, known as Widow Shao, was very hospitable.

Thus, a friend called for a wine boat, the larger one named "Heng," and the smaller one named "Shagu boat," hosting us as the hosts. He let me choose a courtesan, and I chose a young one, whose figure and appearance resembled my wife Yun Niang, with slender feet. Her name was Xier. Xiu Feng called another courtesan named Cuigu. Everyone else had their previous favorites. Each of us took our chosen courtesans, set them in the middle of the boat, and began to drink heartily. By the time it was past midnight, I was worried that I couldn't control myself and decided to return to the residence within the city. However, the city gate had been closed for a long time. It turned out that in coastal cities, the gates closed at sunset, something I was unaware of.

When the banquet ended, some were lying down eating opium, some were joking with their courtesans. The servants on the courtesan boats brought pillows and quilts for everyone, preparing the beds. I privately asked Xier, "Can we stay on this boat?" She said, "There are cabins available for accommodation, but I don't know if there will be guests tonight." The so-called cabin was the attic on the top of the boat.

I said, "Let's go and take a look." I called for a small boat and sailed to the side of Widow Shao's boat. The entire Yang gang courtesan boat was arranged like a corridor with lights. Fortunately, there were no guests in the boat tower. The madam welcomed us with a smile and said, "I knew there were distinguished guests today, so I left the boat tower waiting." I laughed and said, "Madam, you are truly a fairy under the lotus leaf." Then, a servant held a candle in front to lead the way, and we climbed the ladder to the boat tower from the back of the cabin. The boat tower was like a small room, with a long couch on one side, and a table and chairs on the side.

Opening the curtain and going further inside, we reached the head cabin at the top, where the bed was also arranged on the side. In the middle was a square window fitted with glass, no fire was burning, but the room was brightly lit because of the lights on the opposite boat. Inside, the bedding, curtains, and boxes were all exquisite.

Xier said, "You can look up at the moon from the platform." She folded open a window above the ladder, leading to the top of the stern. Three sides were equipped with short railings, but you could see the bright moon in the night sky and the vast water and sky, quite magnificent. Among the crisscrossing boats, which looked like floating leaves on the water, were rows of wine boats, shining like stars in the sky. Along with the bustling sounds of small boats shuttling back and forth, the music of the flute and strings, mixed with the sound of the rising tide, evoked fluctuating emotions.

I said, "This is what they mean by 'Youth doesn't enter Guang,' right now!" Unfortunately, my wife Yun Niang couldn't come here with me. Looking back at Xier, she vaguely resembled Yun Niang under the moonlight. Therefore, I took her arm and left the platform, entering the cabin, extinguishing the candles, and accompanying her to sleep. When dawn was about to break, Xiu Feng and the others had already arrived, laughing and joking. I put on my clothes to greet them, and everyone blamed me for running away last night. I said, "There was no other reason, I just feared you would uncover the blankets." Then, we all returned to the residence within the city.

A few days later, Xiu Feng and I visited the Haizhu Temple together.

The temple was situated on an island in the water, with walls resembling a fortress, about five feet above the water on all sides. There were caves on the walls, with cannons mounted to guard against sea pirates. As the tide rose and fell, the line of sight fluctuated with the water, making it impossible to determine whether the cannons were rising or falling, which was the unpredictability of physics. The Thirteen Foreign Firms were on the west side of Youlan Gate, with houses structured like Western-style houses. Across the river was a place called Huadi, with a variety of flowers and trees, which was a place in Guangzhou where flowers were sold. I thought I knew every kind of flower, but I only recognized six or seven here, asking about some flower names, some of which were not recorded in the "Compendium of Flowers." Perhaps it was due to different local pronunciations?

The scale of Haizhu Temple was extremely large, with banyan trees planted inside the mountain gate. Some were over ten meters in circumference, providing dense shade like a car roof, never withering even in autumn and winter. The pillars, rails, windows, and screens of the halls were all made of iron pear wood. There were also Bodhi trees, with leaves shaped like lungs. After soaking in water and removing the bark, the flesh inside was as delicate as cicada wings, suitable for making small pages to transcribe scriptures.

On the way back, we visited the courtesan boat to see Xier. Coincidentally, neither Cuigu nor Xier had any guests. After finishing tea, we were preparing to leave, but the two of them insisted on keeping us for a while longer. I preferred to stay in the boat tower, but the madam's daughter-in-law, Daguniang, already had guests. So, I said to Widow Shao, "If it's possible to bring these two to our residence, we can talk for a while longer." Widow Shao said, "That's fine." Xiu Feng went back first, instructing the servants to prepare food and drinks. I then brought Cuigu and Xier back to the residence.

As we were chatting and laughing, unexpectedly, Wang Maolao from the county office came without warning, and we ended up drinking together. Just as the wine touched our lips, we suddenly heard loud voices downstairs, indicating that someone was coming upstairs. It turned out that the landlord's nephew, who was always a troublemaker, learned that I had brought courtesans back to the residence, so he brought people to try to extort money from me.

Xiu Feng complained, "This is all because of our momentary indulgence. I really shouldn't have followed suit!"

I said, "Since things have come to this, it's best to quickly think of a way to retreat. Now is not the time for arguing."

Wang Maolao said, "Let me go downstairs and persuade them first."

I immediately called for servants and quickly hired two sedan chairs, allowing the two prostitutes to escape first before figuring out a way to leave the city. Hearing that Wang Maolao's persuasion downstairs was ineffective, he didn't come upstairs. By this time, the two sedan chairs were ready. My servants were quite agile, leading the way with me in front, Xiu Feng supporting Cuigu, and I supporting Xier at the back, and we all rushed out together. With the help of my servants, Xiu Feng and Cuigu had already left. Xier was grabbed by someone, so I quickly lifted my leg and kicked the person's arm, causing him to let go, and Xier escaped. I also took advantage of the situation to escape.

My servants remained guarding at the door to prevent the ruffians from chasing and robbing us. I hurriedly asked him, "Did you see Xier?" The servant said, "Cuigu has already left in the sedan chair, but I only saw Xier coming out, I didn't see her getting into the sedan chair." I quickly lit a torch and saw that the sedan chair was empty, still by the roadside.

I hurriedly chased to Jinghai Gate. Seeing Xiu Feng standing beside Cuigu's sedan chair, I asked him if he had seen Xier's whereabouts. He replied, "Perhaps she should have run east, but instead she ran to the west!" I hurriedly turned back and passed by more than ten households where I heard someone quietly calling my name in the darkness. When the torch illuminated, it turned out to be Xier. So, I put her in the sedan chair and had sedan bearers carry her on their shoulders. Xiu Feng also caught up and said, "There is a water tunnel near Youlan Gate that can lead out of the city! The locks have been bribed to open. Cuigu has already left, Xier should go there as soon as possible!" I said, "You quickly return to the residence and withdraw, Cuigu and Xier will be handed over to me!"

When we arrived at the edge of the water tunnel, the lock was indeed already open. Cuigu was already waiting there. So, I hugged Xier on one side, Cuigu on the other, and bent down to walk out of the water tunnel with unsteady steps. It was drizzling lightly from the sky, and the road was slippery, making it difficult to walk as if on an oil road. By the riverbank, there was a lively scene on the Sha Men side. Some people on small boats recognized Cuigu and called for us to board their boat. It was only then that I took a closer look at Xier. Her hair was disheveled like flying weeds, and her hairpins and earrings were all gone. I asked, "Were they snatched away by the ruffians?" Xier smiled and said, "I heard that these items were all made of pure gold, which belonged to Aunt. I had already removed them and hidden them in my pocket when I came downstairs. If they were snatched away, it would be a loss for you." I was very impressed by her words, so I let her rearrange her hairpins and earrings, admonishing her not to tell Aunt and using the excuse that my residence was crowded with people, which was why we returned to the boat on Sha Men. Cuigu told Aunt about this and said, "We have already eaten and drunk enough, just prepare some porridge."

At this time, the guests on the boat had already left. Madam Shao ordered Cuigu to accompany me to the boat tower. I noticed that both of their embroidered shoes were soaked and dirty. The three of us ate porridge together and chatted to satisfy our hunger. Then, we talked for a long time under the candlelight and learned that Cuigu's family was from Hunan, while Xier's family was from Henan, with the original surname of Ouyang. Her father had passed away, and her mother had remarried, and she was sold to the brothel by her evil uncle. Cuigu told me about the bitterness of welcoming the new year and bidding farewell to the old: pretending to be happy when she wasn't, drinking more than she could handle, forcing herself to accompany guests when she wasn't feeling well, and singing even when her throat was sore. Moreover, some unruly guests would become aggressive if they were slightly dissatisfied, shouting and cursing loudly. If Aunt didn't understand the situation, she would blame them for not being hospitable enough. There were also guests who liked to harass them all night long, causing distress to their bodies. Xier was still young and new here, so Aunt was still sympathetic to her. Cuigu's words were filled with tears. Xier also silently shed tears.

I hugged Xier and comforted her. I told Cuigu to sleep on the outside bed because she was Xiu Feng's favorite. From then on, sometimes ten days, sometimes five days, Xier would send someone to invite me. Sometimes she would come by boat herself to meet me at the riverbank. Every time I went, I would go with Xiu Feng, not inviting other guests or calling for another courtesan boat. In just one night, I spent four silver coins. Xiu Feng now frequented Cuigu and was often referred to as "jumping ship"; sometimes he even called for two courtesans at once. I, on the other hand, only favored Xier.

Occasionally, I would go alone, either drinking on the platform or chatting on the boat deck, without asking her to sing or forcing her to drink too much alcohol, being affectionate and considerate, making all the courtesans on the boat feel comfortable and content. The surrounding courtesans were all envious of Xier. Whenever there were idle courtesans without guests, knowing that I was on the boat deck, they would definitely come here to inquire. Throughout the entire Yang gang courtesan boat, there was not one who did not know me; every time I boarded their boat, the sound of my name being called was endless. I was overwhelmed by all the attention and couldn't handle it, something that even extravagant spending couldn't achieve.

I spent four months in Lingnan, spending more than one hundred silver coins in total, enjoying the fresh lychees and fruits, which could be considered one of the joys of my life. Later, the madam wanted to extort five hundred silver coins from me and force me to take Xier as a concubine, so I decided to return to my hometown to avoid her harassment. Xiu Feng was infatuated with the local charm, so he persuaded him to buy a courtesan house before we returned to the Wu region via the original route.

The next year, Xiu Feng went to Guangdong again, but my father didn't allow me to go with him, so I accepted the invitation from Qingpu's Yang Prefect. After Xiu Feng returned, he told me that Xier had almost committed suicide because I didn't go to her. Alas! This is also "half a year's dream of the Yang gang, winning the name of the flower boat" ah.

After returning from eastern Guangdong, I worked as a staff officer in Qingpu for two years, without any leisurely trips to talk about. Soon, Yun Niang met Hanyuan, causing much discussion, and Yun fell ill due to anger. I and Cheng Mo'an opened a calligraphy and painting shop on the side of the door to make up for the expenses of medicine and herbs.

Two days after the Mid-Autumn Festival, Wu Yunk'e, Mao Yixiang, and Wang Xingcan invited me to visit Xishan Xiaojing Pavilion. I happened to be busy at the time, so I let them go first. Wu Yunk'e said, "If you can leave the city, meet us at Laihe An in front of the mountain bridge tomorrow at noon." I agreed.

The next day, I left Cheng Mo'an to guard the shop, and I walked out of Changmen alone. When I reached the front of the mountain, I crossed the water bridge, walked along the ridge to the west, and saw a south-facing temple, with a clear river in front of the gate. I knocked on the door and asked, and the response came, "Where does the guest come from?" I told him. He smiled and replied, "This is 'De Yun An', didn't you see the plaque? Laihe An has already passed!" I said, "I didn't see any temple from the water bridge to here." The man turned back and pointed, saying, "Don't you see the dense bamboo forest in the earthen wall? That's it."

So I returned the way I came, arrived at the foot of the earthen wall, and found the small door closed. Peeking through the crack in the door, I saw a short hedge and a winding path, with lush green bamboo and quietness without any sound of people. Knocking on the door yielded no response. A passerby said, "There is a stone in the hole in the wall that you can use to knock on the door." I tentatively knocked a few times, and sure enough, a young novice came out to answer. I followed the path, crossed a small stone bridge, turned west, and only then did I see the mountain gate. Hanging above was a black lacquered plaque, with the words "Laihe" written in gold powder, followed by a long inscription, but I didn't have time to read it in detail.

After entering the gate, I passed by the Great Hall of Skanda Bodhisattva. The hall was clean and dust-free, knowing that this was the Xiaojing Pavilion. Suddenly, I saw a little novice coming out of the corridor on the left with a teapot. I shouted to inquire, and heard Wang Xingcan laughing and saying, "How about it? I said Sanbai would never break his promise, right?" Then Wu Yunk'e came out to welcome me, saying, "We were waiting for you to have breakfast. Why did you come so late?"

A monk followed behind him, bowing to me and asking where I came from. After we entered the Xiaojing Pavilion, there were only three small rooms, with a plaque inscribed with the words "Guixuan". Two osmanthus trees in the courtyard were in full bloom. Wang Xingcan and Mao Yixiang stood up and shouted, "Three cups for being late!" At the banquet, there were exquisite dishes, both vegetarian and meat, and a variety of wines. I asked them, "How many places did you visit?" Wu Yunk'e said, "We only went to Deyun and Heting this morning because it was late when we arrived yesterday." We gathered together and drank for a long time.

After dinner, we set off from Deyun and Heting again and visited eight or nine places, ending at Huashan. Each place had its own charm, which cannot all be described. At the top of Huashan, there is a Lotus Peak, but since it was late, we agreed to visit again in the future. The osmanthus flowers were lush and beautiful here; we went to the osmanthus tree and each drank a cup of clear tea before taking a sedan chair down the mountain and returning directly to Laihe An.

To the east of Guixuan, there is another small pavilion called Linjie Xiao Ge, where cups and plates were already arranged. Although Monk Zhuyi was silent, he was hospitable and good at drinking. At first, we used osmanthus flowers as wine orders, and then each person performed a wine order until the second watch before stopping.

I said, "The moonlight is so beautiful tonight, it's a waste to sleep without enjoying it. I wonder if there is a spacious place somewhere where we can admire the moon and not waste this fine night!" Monk Zhuyi said, "You can ascend to the Fanghe Pavilion."

Wu Yunk'e said, "Since Xingcan brought his zither, why don't we go there and have him play? We haven't heard his wonderful music yet." So we all went together.

Amidst the fragrance of osmanthus, amidst the frost-covered forest, under the moonlit sky, everything was silent. Xingcan played "Three Movements of Plum Blossoms" with enthusiasm, giving people a feeling of floating and transcending. Yixiang was also inspired, taking out an iron flute from his sleeve and playing it softly.

Yun Ke said, "Those who watch the moon tonight at Shihu Lake cannot be as happy as us." On August 18th in Suzhou, there was a grand event of watching the moon under the Chunqiao Bridge at Shihu Lake. Every year at this time, pleasure boats crowded together, and there was music and singing throughout the night. The event was ostensibly to watch the moon, but in reality, it was just about drinking and revelry with courtesans.

Soon, as the moon set and the frost grew cold, everyone returned home contentedly and stayed overnight at the Xiaojing Pavilion on West Mountain.

The next morning, Wu Yun Ke said to everyone, "There is a place here called Wuyin An, which is extremely elegant and secluded. Have any of you been there before?"

Everyone replied, "Not only have we not been there, we haven't even heard of it."

The monk Zhu Yi said, "Wuyin An is surrounded by mountains on all four sides, and it is quite remote. Many monks cannot live here for long. I went there one year, and the temple was already in ruins. Since the layman Chen Mupeng repaired it, I haven't been back. I vaguely remember the route. If you all want to visit, I'm willing to be your guide."

Yi Xiang asked, "Are we going on an empty stomach?"

The monk Zhu Yi smiled and said, "I have prepared vegetarian noodles. Let one layman carry the utensils and follow along."

After everyone finished the vegetarian noodles, they set off on foot. Passing by Gaoyi Garden, Wu Yun Ke wanted to visit the Baiyun Monastery. When they arrived at the monastery and sat down, a monk walked out slowly and greeted Yun Ke with a bow, asking, "It's been two months since I last saw you. Is there any news in the city? Is the commander still in the camp?" Suddenly, Yi Xiang stood up and shouted, "Baldy!" then left in a huff. I and Xingcan suppressed our laughter and followed suit. Yun Ke and the monk exchanged pleasantries for a few moments before bidding farewell and leaving.

Gaoyi Garden is the tomb of Fan Wenzheng, right next to the Baiyun Monastery. There is a pavilion facing a rocky cliff, with vines hanging above and a small pond below. This place is called Boyu Tan. They brewed tea with a bamboo stove, and the place was extremely secluded. Unfortunately, the monks were vulgar, and we couldn't bear to stay for long.

At this moment, passing through Shangsha Village and Chicken Cage Mountain, we arrived at the place where Hong Gan and I used to climb high. The scenery was as it was in the past, but Hong Gan was no longer there, which filled me with emotions. Just as I was feeling melancholy, we were suddenly blocked by a stream, unable to continue. Three or five village children were digging mushrooms in the weeds nearby. They looked at us curiously and laughed, as if surprised by why so many people had come here. When we asked them for directions to Wuyin An, they said, "The water ahead is too strong to cross. Go back a few steps, and there's a small path to the south. Cross over the mountain ridge, and you'll get there."

Following the children's advice, we crossed over the mountain ridge and walked for more than a mile to the south. Gradually, we found ourselves surrounded by dense bamboo and towering mountains, with lush greenery and no traces of human activity.

Monk Zhu Yi hesitated and looked around, saying, "It seems to be here, but the road is hard to discern. What should we do?" I crouched down and looked closely, vaguely seeing a dilapidated stone wall among the bamboo forest. I pushed aside the bamboo, crossed over, and found a door with the inscription "Wuyin Chan Temple, rebuilt by Mr. Peng on such and such date."

Everyone exclaimed in joy, "If you weren't here, this place would have become Wulingyuan today!"

The mountain gate was tightly closed, and despite knocking for a long time, no one responded. Suddenly, there was a creaking sound from the side, and a small door opened. A young man in patched robes, with a yellow complexion and worn-out shoes, came out and asked, "What brings you here, guests?" Monk Zhu Yi greeted him and said, "We admire the tranquility of this place and have come to visit." The young man said, "This poor mountain temple, the monks have all left, and there's no one to receive guests. Please go elsewhere for sightseeing." With that, he prepared to close the door.

Wu Yun Ke hurriedly stopped him and promised to reward him for opening the door for us to visit, but the young man smiled and said, "We don't even have tea leaves here; I'm just worried about neglecting guests. There's no need for rewards." With the mountain gate open, we saw the Buddha statue inside, shining with golden light amidst the green shade.

The stone foundation in the courtyard was covered with moss, and the steps behind the hall were as steep as a wall, surrounded by stone railings. To the west of the hall, there was a stone resembling a steamed bun, about two zhang tall, with young bamboo planted around it. Turning west from the hall, there were three guest halls facing a large stone. Behind the stone, there was a small moon pond with clear spring water flowing, and aquatic plants floating. To the east of the guest halls was the main hall, and to the left of the hall, heading west, were the monks' quarters and kitchen. Behind the hall was a steep cliff, with dense trees casting thick shade, and one could not see the sky when looking up.

Xingcan was quite tired, leaning against the edge of the pond to rest. I also leaned against the edge of the pond, about to open the wine utensils for a small drink, when suddenly I heard Yi Xiang's voice coming from the treetops, shouting, "San Bai, come quickly! There's a wonderful scenery here." Looking up, I couldn't see anyone, so I followed Xingcan to search for him. We went out through a small door in the east wing room and walked north, with stone steps like ladders. Inadvertently, we saw a building in the bamboo grove and climbed up along the steps. On the top floor, eight windows were wide open, with a plaque inscribed with the words "Feiyun Ge." The surrounding mountains embraced the building like a fortress, with only one corner missing in the southwest, where the water met the sky, and sailboats could be faintly seen on the vast Taihu Lake! Leaning against the window and looking down, the wind blew through the bamboo tops, creating waves like wheat. Yi Xiang said, "How do you feel?" I said, "This is indeed a rare and wonderful place." Suddenly, we heard Yun Ke shouting from the west side of the building, "Yi Xiang, come quickly! There's an even more extraordinary scenery here!"

So we went downstairs again and headed west, climbing a dozen steps before the scenery suddenly opened up, flat like a stone platform. I estimated that this place was already above the cliff behind the hall, with remnants of broken bricks and stones, probably the foundation of the old hall. Standing here, surrounded by mountains, it was even more refreshing than Feiyun Ge. Yi Xiang faced Taihu Lake and let out a long roar, which was echoed by the mountains. So we all sat on the ground, opened the wine, and suddenly felt hungry. The young man wanted to cook porridge instead of tea, so we asked him to make porridge instead and invited him to eat with us.

When asked why the place was so deserted, he said, "There are no neighbors around, and bandits often come at night. When it's harvest time, robbers come as well. Even if we plant vegetables and fruits, they are mostly picked by woodcutters. This is the lower courtyard of Chongning Temple. The head chef of Chongning Temple sends one stone of rice cakes and a jar of pickles every midmonth. I am a descendant of the Peng family and temporarily look after this place. I'm about to leave soon, and soon there will be no one here." Yun Ke gave him a piece of silver as a reward.

When we returned to Laihe An, we hired a boat to go home. Upon returning, I painted a picture of "Wuyin" and gave it to Monk Zhu Yi as a souvenir of this joyful trip.

That winter, I was implicated in guaranteeing loans for friends, which caused discord in my family, so I stayed with the Hua family in Xishan.

In the spring of the second year, I planned to seek employment in Yangzhou but was short of money. A friend, Han Chunquan, held a position in Shangyang Prefecture, so I went to visit him. At that time, I was shabby and couldn't enter the government office, so I arranged to meet him in the county temple garden pavilion. When my old friend Han Chunyu came out to meet me and realized my distress, he generously gave me ten taels of silver. The county temple garden was built with donations from Western merchants and was extremely spacious, but unfortunately, the various scenic spots were arranged haphazardly, and the artificial hills built behind were unevenly distributed.

On the way back, I suddenly remembered the magnificent scenery of Yushan. There happened to be a convenient boat, so I boarded it and went to Yushan. It was early spring, with peach and plum blossoms competing in beauty. I was alone on the journey and felt troubled by the lack of companionship, so I brought three hundred copper coins and leisurely arrived at Yushan Academy. Looking up from outside the wall, I saw clusters of trees and flowers, with charming red and green colors, close to the water and near the mountains, extremely picturesque. Unfortunately, I couldn't find the entrance, so after asking for directions, I arrived at a small tea shop with a tent set up, where I sat down. The Biluo Chun tea brewed in the shop was excellent. When I asked the owner where the best scenery in Yushan was, a traveler said, "Go out from here through the west gate, near Jianmen, is the best scenery of Yushan. If you want to go, I'm willing to be your guide." I happily accepted his suggestion.

After leaving the west gate and following the foot of the mountain, we walked up and down for about a few miles, gradually seeing towering peaks with horizontal grain lines. When we arrived at the foot of the mountain, the mountain split in two, with uneven cliffs on both sides, tens of meters high. Approaching and looking up, the cliffs seemed to be about to collapse. The man said, "It is said that there is a place where immortals live on the top, with many scenic spots related to immortals. Unfortunately, we didn't find the way to visit." Feeling inspired, I rolled up my sleeves and climbed up like an ape, reaching the top of the mountain directly.

The so-called immortal dwelling place was only about ten feet deep, with a crack in the roof that allowed one to see the sky. Looking down, my legs grew weak, and I nearly fell. So I turned my belly towards the stone wall, tightly grasped the vine, and descended. The man exclaimed, "Wow! Your adventurous spirit is unparalleled; I have never seen anyone like you." Feeling thirsty, I invited the man to a roadside inn for three cups of wine. Even as the sun was setting, we couldn't fully explore Yushan, so I picked up a dozen pieces of red stones and carried them back with me. Then, with my belongings on my back, I took a night boat back to Suzhou, while the man returned to Xishan. It was a pleasant journey amidst the sorrows of my life.

In the spring of the Jiaqing year (1804), I was deeply saddened by the death of my father. In my grief, I planned to leave home and wander afar, but my friend Xia Yishan persuaded me to stay at his house. In August of that autumn, he invited me to go to Yongtai Sha in Donghai to collect interest. Yongtai Sha belonged to Chongming Island, more than a hundred miles away from the mouth of the Liu

River. It was a new island formed by the accumulation of tidal sands, with no streets or markets yet. We saw vast reeds and few people, except for dozens of warehouses belonging to the Ding family, who were in the same line of business as Xia Yishan. They dug ditches and built embankments around, planting willows on top.

The Ding family, with the surname Ding Shi Chu, hailed from Chongming Island and was the largest landowner in Yongtai Sha. Their accountant, surnamed Wang, was hospitable and unceremonious. When we first met, we became fast friends. They slaughtered a pig for the meal, and we drank from a large jar of wine. When playing drinking games, they used their thumbs instead of fingers and didn't understand poetry or literature. Their singing was just shouting, with no regard for musical rhythm. When the wine was strong, they directed workers to box and wrestle for entertainment. They kept over a hundred bulls, all spending the night on the embankments. They raised geese as a signal against pirates. Every day, they drove hawks and dogs through the reeds and sandbanks, often catching many birds. I followed behind, running and resting when tired.

They led me to the fields where the crops were ripe. Each field was surrounded by high embankments to prevent flooding. There were water passages on the embankments, managed by water gates. During droughts, they opened the gates at high tide for irrigation, and during floods, they opened them at low tide for drainage. The tenants lived scattered around like stars, gathering at a single call from the landlord. They referred to the landlord as "Master," obedient and sincere. But if angered by injustice, they were rougher than wolves and tigers. Fortunately, fairness and justice prevailed, and they immediately complied with what was right.

Watching the wind and rain on the fields felt like being in ancient times. Lying in bed and looking out, it seemed like waves of the sea, with the sound of the tides near the pillow, resembling the drums of war on the battlefield. One night, I suddenly saw red lights shining tens of miles away, huge like bamboo baskets floating on the sea, and the red glow reflected in the sky, resembling a fire. Shi Chu said, "This is the appearance of divine lights and fires; new sand fields will emerge soon!" Xia Yishan was always bold, but here, he was even more unrestrained. I was also uninhibited, singing loudly on the backs of bulls and dancing in the fields, enjoying this truly carefree journey.

After completing Xia Yishan's business, we returned to Suzhou in October.

In my hometown of Suzhou, the most beautiful scenery was first at Qianqingyun behind the Huqiu Mountain, followed by Jianchi. The others relied heavily on artificial elements, tainted with cosmetics, and had long lost the original appearance of mountains and forests. Even the newly built Baigong Temple and Tianying Bridge were just named for elegance. As for Yifang Bin, I renamed it Wildflowers Bin, resembling women adorned with makeup, only outwardly charming.

The most famous Lion Grove in the city, although attributed to Ni Yunlin and with its exquisite rocks and ancient trees, appeared as if randomly piled coal; some moss added, some caves chiseled, lacking the natural momentum of mountains and forests. From my limited observation, I couldn't appreciate its beauty.

Lingyan Mountain, the former site of the Wu King's Palace, had several scenic spots such as Xishi Shrine, Xiangxielang, and Caixiang Path, but they lacked cohesion and spaciousness, inferior to the secluded charm of Tianping Mountain and Zhixing Mountain.

Dengwei Mountain, also known as Yuan Tomb, with Taihu Lake to the west and Jin Feng to the east, had vermilion cliffs and green pavilions, resembling a painting. Those who lived here made a living by planting plum blossoms. When the flowers bloomed, the surrounding area looked like a vast expanse of white snow, hence the name "Fragrant Snow Sea."

To the left of the mountain were four ancient cypress trees named "Qing," "Qi," "Gu," and "Guai." The one named "Qing" had a straight trunk, flourishing like an emerald canopy; the one named "Qi" lay horizontally on the ground, with three bends resembling the character "之"; the one named "Gu" had no branches or leaves at the top, flat and broad like a palm, already decayed into a palm-shaped stump; the one named "Guai" had a twisted body like a spinning top. Legend has it that they were all planted before the Han Dynasty.

In the spring of the Yi Chou year, Xia Yishan's father, Mr. Chunxiang, and his brother Jieshi, led four of their sons to pay their respects at the ancestral shrine on Fusang Mountain and sweep the tombs, inviting me to join them. On the way, we first visited Lingyan Mountain, then crossed the Tiger Mountain Bridge, and entered the Fragrant Snow Sea to admire the plum blossoms. The ancestral shrine of Fusang Mountain was hidden in the Fragrant Snow Sea; at that time, the plum blossoms were in full bloom, and even speaking felt like breathing in fragrance. I once painted twelve volumes of "Fusang Wind and Wood" for Jieshi.

In September of that year, I followed Shizhuotang to Sichuan Chongqing for official duties.

Going upstream along the Yangtze River, the boat arrived at Wancheng. At the foot of Wanshan, there was the tomb of the loyal minister Yu Que from the Yuan Dynasty, with three halls next to it called "Daguan Pavilion," facing the South Lake and backed by Qianshan. The pavilion was situated halfway up the mountain, offering a panoramic view of the distant scenery. Next to it was a long corridor, with windows open to the north, the frosty leaves turning red, vibrant like peach and plum blossoms. The companions were Jiang Shoupeng and Cai Ziqin.

Outside the southern city was a Wang family garden. It was long from east to west and short from north to south, probably because it was close to the city wall in the north and bordered by a lake in the south. When the terrain constrained the garden, it was quite difficult to manage and arrange. However, I observed its structure, which adopted the method of stacking terraces and pavilions. The so-called stacked terraces had moon platforms on the roofs as courtyards, with rocks and flowers planted on them, making people unaware of the houses below their feet. The places where rocks were stacked on top were filled below, while the places where courtyards were above remained hollow, allowing the plants to grow with earth energy. The so-called stacked pavilions were pavilions on the upper floors, with platforms above the pavilions. They spiraled up and down, overlapping into four layers. There was even a small pond on the upper floor, with no water leakage; I couldn't even guess which part was hollow and which part was solid. Its foundation was entirely built of bricks and stones, with weight-bearing areas imitating the Western column method. Fortunately, the courtyard faced the South Lake, with an unobstructed view, making it more enjoyable than gardens on flat ground. Truly a marvel of artificial beauty.

Wuchang Yellow Crane Tower stood on Huanghu Ji, behind which was Yellow Crane Mountain, commonly known as Snake Mountain. The tower had three floors, with painted beams and flying eaves, towering against the city and facing the Han River, opposite to the Qingchuan Pavilion in Hanyang.

Braving the snow, I climbed the tower with Shizhuotang, overlooking the vast sky, with snowflakes swirling around, pointing afar at the silver mountains and jade trees, feeling as if in a fairyland. Small boats traversed the river, sails fluttering in the wind, like giant waves rolling and sweeping away bits of fallen leaves; any desire for fame and wealth faded at this moment. There were many inscriptions on the walls, and although I couldn't remember many, I recall one pair of couplets:

"When will the Yellow Crane return, let's drink from the golden cups together, watering the thousand-year-old grass of the Yangtze River;

But all we see is the white clouds flying away, and who else will blow the jade flute, in May's plum blossoms of the river city."

Chi Bi, located outside the Han Chuan Gate of the prefectural city, stood tall by the river, with steep cliffs resembling walls. The stones were all red, hence the name, as described in the "Shui Jing." Su Dongpo once visited here and wrote two essays, claiming this place was where the Wu and Wei armies battled, which wasn't entirely accurate.

Below Chi Bi, land had emerged, with a two-story pavilion built upon it.

In midwinter of that year, when we arrived in Jingzhou, Shizhuotang received news of his promotion to the position of Observer at Tongguan, so he asked me to stay temporarily in Jingzhou. Thus, I regretted not seeing the mountains and waters of Shu. Shizhuotang's son, Dunfu, along with his family and Cai Ziqin and Xizhitang, also stayed in Jingzhou, living in the abandoned garden of the Liu family. I remember the inscription on the hall of this garden was "Purple Wisteria, Red Tree, Mountain Residence."

Staying as a guest in Jingzhou was free from troubles. Sometimes I sang, sometimes I sang, sometimes I went out, sometimes I talked. At the end of the year, although everyone was not wealthy, there was harmony between upper and lower classes, exchanging clothes for wine, and preparing drums and gongs for music. Every night, there was drinking, and every drinking session had drinking games. Even in hard times, even if it was just two liang of strong liquor, we would still play drinking games to liven up the atmosphere.

While in Jingzhou, I met a fellow surnamed Cai from the same hometown. After discussing our family trees, we found that we were from the same clan, so he acted as a guide to tour the scenic spots.

We went to the Qujiang Tower in front of the Prefectural School. Zhang Jiuling had once composed a poem there when he was the chief secretary. Zhu Xi also wrote a poem about it: "Yearning to look back, let's climb Qujiang Tower together."

On the city wall, there is a majestic Xiongchu Tower, built by the Gao family during the Five Dynasties. It has a grand and towering momentum, offering a distant view of several hundred miles. Surrounding the city wall and along the moat, willows are planted, with small boats paddling back and forth, evoking a poetic atmosphere.

The government office of Jingzhou was once the headquarters of General Guan Yu. Inside the ceremonial gate, there is a green stone trough, which is said to be the feeding trough of the Red Hare horse. I once went to the west of the city to find the former residence of Luo Han but couldn't find it. I also went to the north of the city to find the former residence of Song Yu. In the chaos of the Hou Jing Rebellion, Yu Xin once hid in Jiangling, residing in Song Yu's former residence. However, later the former residence was turned into a tavern, and now it is impossible to identify it.

On New Year's Eve of that year, after the snow stopped, it was extremely cold. Welcoming the spring without the usual New Year's greetings, every day was spent setting off firecrackers, flying kites, and making paper lanterns for fun. Soon, news spread that the wives and children of the scholars were drifting downstream. Dunfu also packed up his belongings and set off with everyone, landing at Fancheng and heading straight to Tongguan.

Heading west from Henan's Wuxiang County, after leaving the Hangu Pass, you can see the words "Purple Qi Coming from the East." This is where Laozi rode the green ox. The road between the two mountains can only accommodate two horses side by side. After walking about ten li from here, you will arrive at Tongguan. With steep cliffs on the left and the Yellow River on the right, Tongguan is built between mountains and rivers, with towering towers and lofty heights. However, today, Tongguan has few carriages and horses, and few people. Han Yu once wrote a poem, "Sunlight shines through the four gates of Tongguan," probably describing its desolate scene.

Below the rank of Observer in the city, there is only one auxiliary official. The Daoist office is located near the north gate of the city, with a garden behind it, stretching about three mu. Two ponds have been dug east and west, with water flowing from outside the southwest wall into the eastern pond, then divided into three waterways: one flows south to the main kitchen for daily use; one flows east into the eastern pond; and one flows north, then turns westward to flow into the western pond through the mouth of a stone dragon, then circulates to the northwest, passes through a spillway gate, turns north at the foot of the city wall, passes through a water tunnel, and flows straight into the Yellow River. The flowing water never stops, giving a refreshing feeling to the ears.

Inside the garden, bamboo trees are lush and shade is dense, making it impossible to see the sky when looking up. There is a pavilion in the western pond, surrounded by lotus flowers. To its east are three south-facing study rooms, with grapevines in front and square stone tables and stools underneath for playing chess and drinking wine; the rest of the area is all chrysanthemum gardens. To the west are three east-facing pavilions, where you can listen to the sound of flowing water; there is a small door on the south side of the pavilions, leading to the inner rooms; below the north window of the pavilions, another small pond has been dug, with a small temple north of the pond, dedicated to the flower deity.

In the middle of the garden, there is a three-story building, adjacent to the north gate and as tall as the city wall. From this building, you can overlook the Yellow River outside the city. North of the Yellow River, the mountains are like screens, already belonging to Shanxi. Between these mountains and rivers, it is truly a magnificent scene!

I lived in the southern part of the garden. The house is shaped like a small boat, with a small hill in the courtyard, where there is a small pavilion from which you can overlook the entire garden. The courtyard is surrounded by lush greenery, free from the summer heat. I named the study "The Unmoored Boat." This is the best residence I have had in my wandering life. Between the small hill, dozens of types of chrysanthemums are planted, but unfortunately, I did not wait for them to bloom. Later, Zhuotang was transferred to Shanxi as a censor. He moved his family to Tongchuan Academy, and I followed to live in the academy.

Zhuotang went to Shandong to take up his new post, and I, along with Ziqin and Tang, had nothing to do, so we went out to play.

One day, we rode horses to Huayin Temple. Passing through Huafengli, you reach the place where Emperor Yao accepted the three sacrifices. There are many Qin junipers and Han cypresses in the temple, most of them three or four embraces; some junipers embrace cypresses, and some cypresses embrace junipers. Inside the temple grounds are many ancient steles, including one with the characters "Fu" and "Shou" written by the ancestor Chen Tuan.

At the foot of Huashan, there is a Yuquan Temple, where Chen Tuan became immortal. There is a stone cave inside, about the size of a room, with a statue of Chen Tuan lying on a stone bed. The water in Yuquan Temple is clear and the sand is bright, with lots of red grass growing, and the spring water flows swiftly, surrounded by bamboo. Outside the stone cave is a square pavilion, with a plaque inscribed with "Wuyou Pavilion." Next to it are three ancient trees, with patterns resembling cracked charcoal, and the leaves are darker than those of locust trees, but I don't know their name. The locals call them "Wuyou Trees." Huashan is thousands of ren high, but unfortunately, I did not bring food to climb it.

On the way back, I saw persimmons ripening in the trees by the roadside, so I picked one while riding on horseback and ate it. The locals shouted to stop me, but I didn't listen to them. After chewing, it tasted extremely bitter, so I quickly spat it out, got off the horse to find spring water to rinse my mouth, before I could speak again. The locals laughed heartily. It turns out that persimmons need to be boiled in water after picking to remove the bitterness, but I didn't know that.

In early October, Zhuotang's family was specially sent by someone from Shandong to pick them up. So, everyone left Tongguan, entered the territory of Henan, and entered the land of Lu. In Jinan Prefecture, Shandong, there is Daming Lake in the west of the city, with many famous attractions such as Lixia Pavilion and Shuixiang Pavilion in the lake. In summer, the shade of willows is dense, and the fragrance of lotus flowers floats in the air. Boating with wine, it is very elegant and leisurely. When I went to see it in winter, I only saw the willows withering and the lake vast.

Baotu Spring is the first of the seventy-two springs in Jinan. The spring water gushes from the ground, boiling up like boiling water. Most springs flow from top to bottom, but this spring flows from bottom to top, which is also a great spectacle. There is a building on the pool, inside which is enshrined a statue of Master Lu Dongbin, and many visitors like to come here to enjoy tea.

In February of the second year, I went to Laiyang, Shandong, to serve as an aide. In the autumn of the Dingmao year, Zhuotang was demoted to a Hanlin, and I followed him to the capital. The so-called "Haishi of Dengzhou" that everyone talked about, I unexpectedly didn't have a chance to see it.

VOLUME FIVE: ZHONGSHAN CHRONICLE

In the fourth year of the Jiaqing reign (1799 AD), which was the year of Siwei in the sexagenary cycle, the King of Ryukyu, Shangmu, passed away. Shangmu's son, Shangzhe, had died seven years earlier; and Shangmu's grandson, Shangwen, submitted a petition to the court requesting to inherit the title and rank of King of Zhongshan. The Chinese court, following a policy of appeasement towards distant small countries, graciously granted Shangwen's request and conducted an assessment during the court deliberations, selecting civil officials as envoys to travel to the Kingdom of Zhongshan.

Zhao Wenkai, Mr. Jieshan, from Taihu Lake, serving as an editor in the Hanlin Academy, was selected as the chief envoy; Mr. Li Dingyuan, Mr. Heshu, from Mianzhou, serving as a scholar in the Imperial Cabinet, was selected as the deputy envoy. Zhao Jieshan sent a quick letter inviting me to accompany him. Due to my elderly parents and fearing to travel far from home, I hesitated. However, considering my twenty years of traveling experience and exploration of many remote and inaccessible places, my knowledge was still limited to a narrow range. I had never seen the landscapes beyond our borders, let alone the vast and beautiful East Sea we were about to traverse. Therefore, after discussing with my father, he agreed to let me go along.

There were a total of five people accompanying the mission: Mr. Wang Wenhao, Mr. Qin Yuanjun, Mr. Miao Song, Mr. Yang Huacai, and myself. On the first day of May in the fifth year of Jiaqing (1800 AD), we set sail with the envoys. Throughout the journey, auspicious sea winds filled the sails, and divine-like fish and shrimp swam on both sides of the ship. After six days and nights, we arrived at our destination.

I meticulously recorded everything I saw. I described the beautiful and rugged landscapes, documented the splendid and bizarre products, recorded the rules and regulations of the government offices, and praised the demeanor and integrity of the gentlemen and ladies. While my writing may not be extraordinary, the events are factual. I am ashamed of my shallow and crude skills, willing to endure ridicule for my shortcomings; what matters most is conveying sincerity, which perhaps surpasses empty words and contrived interpretations.

On the first day of May, which happened to be the summer solstice, we boarded the ship with our luggage and set sail. Traditionally, the envoys appointed to confer the title of King of Zhongshan depart on the summer solstice with the southwest wind and return on the winter solstice with the northeast wind, which is usually reliable. There were two ships, with the chief envoy and the deputy envoy sharing one. The upper part of the ship was seven zhang long, with a hanging stern three zhang long, a depth of one zhang three chi, and a width of two zhang two chi, almost half the size of the traditional envoys' ships. There were masts at the front and back of the ship, each more than six zhang long and three chi thick; the mast in the middle of the front cabin was more than ten zhang long and six chi thick, made of foreign trees. There were a total of twenty-four cabins on the ship, with stones placed at the bottom to maintain stability, carrying over one hundred thousand catties of cargo. A large cannon was placed at the bow of the ship, with two large cannons on each side of the ship, and the rest of the weapons were stored in the cabin. Under the main mast, there was a large wooden pulley for moving the cannons and raising and lowering the sails, which required dozens of people to operate. The deck served as a platform for battle, and the stern tower served as a command post, with flags erected and banners arranged, serving as the envoy's meeting hall. Below the stern tower was the helm room, with a small cabin in front containing maps and compasses. Going down the ladder from the middle cabin, there was a cabin about six chi high, where the envoys gathered for meals. The front cabin stored gunpowder and food, the rear cabin housed the soldiers, followed by the water cabin with four wells. The situation in the second cabin was the same as in the first. There were about two hundred and sixty people on each ship, crowded due to the small size. With the monsoon already arriving, changing to a larger ship would likely delay the departure time.

On the second day, at noon, the ship arrived at Aomen to anchor. At four o'clock in the afternoon, auspicious clouds appeared in the western sky, colorful and round, reflecting each other with the flags on the ship. All the spectators praised its magical auspiciousness. Some of the auspicious clouds resembled black jade, some like white jade; some resembled lingzhi mushrooms, some like jade-like seedlings; some like deep red brocade; some like purple silk; some like the leaves of Wenxing apricot trees, some like peach trees laden with fruit, some like wild grass on the autumn plains, some like the waves of the Xiang River in spring. I had read Tu Changqing's poetry from the Ming Dynasty before, but only now did I realize the subtlety of his descriptions. A painter named Shi created a magnificent painting called "Pleasure of Sailing," which was especially brilliant. After seeing this painting, I dared not pick up my brush again. Although Xiangya was good at painting landscapes, he could not reach the level of "Pleasure of Sailing."

On the fourth day, at ten o'clock in the night, we weighed anchor. Riding the tide, we sailed to Luoxing Pagoda. The sea and sky were boundless. My wife, Yunniang, had said when we traveled to Taihu Lake in the past that seeing the vastness of heaven and earth would make her life worthwhile. If she could see the magnificence of the sea, how joyful would she be?

On the ninth day, at six o'clock in the morning, we saw Pengjia Mountain. Three peaks lined up in a row, with the eastern side higher than the western side. In the evening, we saw Diaoyutai. Three high peaks stood apart like a pen rack, with bare rocks covering the entire mountain. At this time, the sea and sky were unified, and the ship sailed smoothly on the sea surface. Countless white seagulls flew around the ship, seemingly bidding us farewell; we wondered where they had flown from. By nightfall, the shadows of stars crisscrossed the water, and the moonlight was fragmented and shattered, making the entire sea surface appear to be burning with flames, rising and falling with the waves. This was what Mu Hua of the Jin Dynasty referred to as "hidden fires burning" in his "Ode to the Sea."

On the tenth day, at nine o'clock in the morning, the ship arrived at Chiwei Islet. The island was square-shaped, red in color, with raised sides on the east and west, and a depression in the middle, where there were two small mountain peaks. Our ship sailed past the north side of the mountain, where two large fish accompanied us, sandwiching the ship between them as they swam alongside us. Their heads and tails were not visible, only their backs were seen, black with a hint of green, like thick dry logs, leaning against the sides of the ship. The sailors believed that a storm was imminent, and the large fish were escorting us in advance. At noon, a thunderstorm of epic proportions struck, the wind shifted to the northeast, and the rudder became ineffective. The ship spun dangerously, but luckily the two large fish remained close, not leaving yet. Suddenly, a thunderous explosion was heard, and the raging storm abruptly ceased. At four o'clock in the afternoon, the wind shifted to the southwest and grew stronger. Everyone on the ship raised their hands to their foreheads, thinking that divine spirits were aiding us. I wrote two poems to record the scene at the time. The poems wrote:

"Wandering across the waves of Qi Prefecture all my life,
Embarking on a distant journey again with the Star Raft.
The fish untangle danger, the wind shifts in our favor,
Where the sea clouds turn red lies Ryukyu."
"White waves surge, shaking the vast wilderness,
Gazing eastward at the boundless sea and sky.
This journey strengthens the courage of scholars,
Facing wind and thunder with resolute spirit."
I thought I could capture the scene at that time very well.

On the eleventh day, at noon, we saw Mount Gumi from afar. Mount Gumi had eight ridges, each with one or two peaks, some disconnected, some continuous. At three o'clock in the afternoon, a strong wind brought pouring rain, but despite the heavy rain, the wind was favorable. As night fell, the ship approached Mount Gumi. Because there were many hidden reefs near Mount Gumi, the Ryukyu people dared not sail at night and could only wait for daylight to continue. After stopping the ship, there was no need to drop anchor; we simply furled the sails and let the ship float in the waves, unable to retreat. At eight o'clock in the evening, signal torches were raised on the ship, and Mount Gumi responded with torches. After inquiring with knowledgeable individuals, we learned that this was the Ryukyu people's signal: firing cannons during the day and raising torches at night. This was what was referred to as "receiving the signal" in the "Book of Rites."

On the twelfth day, at eight o'clock in the morning, the ship passed by Machishi Mountain. The mountain resembled a mix of dogs and sheep, with four peaks scattered and standing upright, like celestial horses galloping freely. After estimating that we had sailed for another thirteen or fourteen hours, the ship again used the compass to correct its course and entered Naha Port. Looking back, we saw the ships welcoming the envoys following closely behind, and people congratulated each other.

    Looking at historical maritime charts, place names such as Xiaoliuqiu, Jilongsan, and Huangmayu were still on the route, but we didn't see them on this voyage. It is said that the leader of the Ryukyu sailors, who is sixty years old this year, has sailed eight times between the seas, carefully observing each time and deducing the accurate positions. He believed that the position was not in the Chen or Mao hours. In the Heavenly Stems, the position of Yi-Mao is in an odd number, and Yi has a strong magnetic force, so this route was the most direct, and along the way, only three mountains were seen before reaching Mount Gumi. At the start of the voyage, the compass used a single Chen position, and after sailing for seven hours, it switched to a Yi-Chen position, which was used from then on. After passing Mount Gumi, the Yi-Mao position was used. However, it is difficult to calculate the time accurately with just incense sticks. I thought that from the Five Tiger Gate in the capital to the official wharf in Ryukyu, the distance was fixed, so according to the timetable, the distance traveled per hour was about one hundred and ten li. From sailing on the eighth day of the month until the Chen hour of the twelfth day, a total of fifty-eight hours of sailing was calculated. On the tenth day, sailing was halted for two hours due to a storm, and on the night of the eleventh day, three hours were spent halted for fear of running aground. In actuality, fifty-three hours of sailing were conducted, and the calculated distance should have been five thousand eight hundred and thirty li. Taking into account the distance from Mount Gumi to Naha Port, the actual distance traveled on the ocean was over six thousand li. According to the leader of the Ryukyu sailors, when sailing at sea, too little wind means you can't sail, but too much wind is equally problematic. With strong winds come big waves, and the force of the surging waves can block the ship's passage, making it retreat two inches for every inch it moves forward. Only a seven-point wind and five-point waves are most suitable for sailing. Our voyage this time was just like that.

    Crossing the ocean, there has never been such a smooth and successful journey as this one. At this time, the Ryukyu people were driving dozens of single-masted boats, towing our ship with ropes, and holding grand ceremonies to welcome the envoys multiple times. At eight o'clock in the morning, the ship entered Naha Port. Earlier, the second ship had disappeared on the tenth day, and it was only now that we learned it had arrived first. The ships welcoming the envoys also entered the harbor one after another and anchored at the pier in front of the Seaside Temple. The quartermaster said, "There has never been a situation where three ships arrived together before."

At noon, we disembarked and went ashore. All the people of the Kingdom of Zhongshan gathered on both sides of the road to watch. The grandson of the King of Zhongshan, Shangwen, led civil and military officials to greet the imperial decree according to protocol. Shangwen was only seventeen years old, with fair skin and a calm demeanor, displaying grace and elegance. Skilled in calligraphy and painting, he exuded a bit of the atmosphere of Song Xue's work.

According to the "Record of the Kingdom of Zhongshan," during the Sui Dynasty, envoy Yujiqu of the Feathered Cavalry once visited the Kingdom of Zhongshan and saw that the geographical shape of the Kingdom of Zhongshan resembled a winding dragon emerging from the water, hence it was initially called "Liuqiu." In the "History of the Sui Dynasty," it was also called "Li Qiu"; in the "New Book of Tang," it was called "Liu Gui"; in the "History of the Yuan Dynasty," it was recorded as "Li Qiu"; and in the Ming Dynasty, it was called "Ryukyu." The "Record of the Kingdom of Zhongshan" also records that in the first year of the Yuan Dynasty's Yuanhu, the Kingdom of Zhongshan was divided into three major parts, totaling eighteen countries, some of which called themselves Kings of the South Mountain and some called themselves Kings of the North Mountain. I have almost traveled to places like Zhongshan and Nanshan, where even the largest villages are less than two li in size, yet they are still called countries. Isn't that exaggerating too much?

The people of Ryukyu often refer to strong winds as typhoons or hurricanes. Based on the poetry of Han Yu, "forcing a hurricane" implies equivalence to a hurricane. According to the "Yupian," a dictionary from ancient China, a "颶" refers to a strong wind. It might be a mistake in the "History of the Tang Dynasty" to mention "海道," which could be an error made by the Ryukyu people. The "History of the Sui Dynasty" mentions tigers, wolves, bears, and leopards on Ryukyu Island, which is no longer the case. It also states the absence of cattle, sheep, donkeys, and horses, with the exception of donkeys. However, there is a variety of livestock available. This teaches us not to fully trust what is written in books.

The Tianxi Embassy faces west and is built in the style of Chinese official offices. Two flagpoles stand in front of the gate, bearing yellow flags with the emperor's decree appointing the king of Zhongshan. There is a reflection wall outside the gate, with two outer doors on the east and west sides, each accompanied by a drum pavilion and a duty room. The gate bears the inscription "Tianxi Embassy," and inside, there are four galleries on each side. The plaque above the welcoming gate reads "Tianze Gate," inscribed by the previous envoy, Mr. Xia Baoguang, though the inscription is now somewhat faded, having been retouched by the former envoy, Mr. Xu Baoguang. On both sides of the gate, there are eleven rooms, with a corridor in the middle. To the west of the corridor, there is a banyan tree planted by Mr. Xu Baoguang himself, with a trunk so large it takes ten people to encircle it. The kitchen is located furthest to the west. The main hall consists of five rooms, with the plaque reading "Fuming Hall," inscribed by the previous envoy, Mr. Wang Ji. To the north, there is a plaque inscribed by Mr. Xu Baoguang reading "Huanglun Sanxi." Behind the main hall, there is a passage leading to the second hall. The second hall also consists of five rooms, with the central room serving as a dining area for the main and deputy envoys. The plaque inscribed by the previous envoy, Mr. Zhou, reads "Shengjiao Dongjian." The rooms on the left and right are bedrooms. Behind the second hall, there are two buildings to the north and south. The southern building serves as the residence for the main envoy, with a plaque inscribed by Mr. Wang Ji reading "Changfeng Pavilion." The northern building serves as the residence for the deputy envoy, with a plaque inscribed by the previous envoy, Mr. Lin Lin, reading "Tingyun Building." To the north of the plaque, there are poetry plaques inscribed by Mr. Haishan. The perimeter is enclosed by polished coral stone walls, resembling a fortress. The walls are covered with phoenix trees, with square trunks devoid of flowers but filled with thorns, resembling whips. The leaves are similar to fire-preventing grass, and locals call them "Jiguluo." There is a well in the courtyard to the south. The roofs of the buildings are covered with tiles, and the ground is paved with square bricks, making the courtyard resemble a beach. The tables, chairs, beds, and curtains inside the embassy are all modeled after Chinese styles. During this period, I wrote four poems, expressing the true sentiments and scenes of the time.

  Confucius Temple is located in Qumi Village. The temple consists of three rooms, with a deity statue in the middle wearing a crown and holding a jade tablet, with the plaque reading "Holy Teacher Confucius." On both sides, there are shrines where two attendants stand holding scriptures, representing the "Four Books" of the Chinese classics. Outside the temple is a platform extending east to west, with stone steps leading up to it. There is a fence resembling a lattice gate, with a military-style gate in the middle to restrict access. The platform overlooks the sea to the east and is surrounded by a seawall. To the east of the temple is the Minglun Hall, where the shrine of Xia Qi is enshrined. The village's elite receive education here, with knowledgeable individuals serving as their teachers. These individuals are paid annually for their services, following Chinese customs. I composed a poem with reverence: "Fame spreads far and wide, revered even in distant lands. Temples solemn, banners noble, teachings divine, embracing all."

Many temples in Zhongshan Kingdom, with Yuanjue Temple being the largest, are visited. At the Liantang Bridge, there is a pavilion where the goddess of eloquence, Doumu, is worshipped. Just before entering, there is a pool called "Yuanjian," surrounded by water plants and lotus flowers. The temple gate is tall and spacious, resembling open wings. Four Vajra guardians stand on either side of the Buddha statue, roughly following the Chinese model. The Buddha hall has seven rooms, and further inside, the main hall also has seven rooms, named "Longyuan Hall." In the middle is the Buddha hall, with shrines on either side for ancestral spirits and the kings of Zhongshan, as well as for the gods. To the left is the abbot's seat, and to the right are seats for worshippers, all equipped with cushions. The area around the seats is covered with neatly folded cloth known as "Tajiaomian." In front of the abbot's seat is the Penglai Courtyard. To the left is the incense kitchen, with a well nearby named "Buleng Spring." To the right of the guest seat is Gulingling, with bizarre rocks scattered among ancient pine trees. To the left are monks' dormitories, and to the right are lion dens. To the south of the monks' quarters is the Music Tower, and to the south of that is a garden filled with flowers, plants, and trees. This is an overview of the magnificent scenery of Yuanjue Temple.

There is also Huguo Temple, where the king prays for rain. Inside the shrine is a deity statue, dark and naked with a fierce expression, holding a sword. There is a bell in the temple, cast in the seventh year of the Jingtai era of the Ming Dynasty (1456 AD). Behind the temple, there are many cycads, also known as iron trees. There is also

Tianwang Temple, where the bell was also cast in the seventh year of the Jingtai era. Then there is Dinghai Temple, where the bell was cast in the third year of the Tianshun era of the Ming Dynasty (1459 AD). However, temples like Longdu Temple, Shanxing Temple, and Heguang Temple have fallen into disrepair and hold no notable significance.

The seafood of Zhongshan Kingdom includes many specialties rarely seen in China. There is a type of stonefish, resembling an octopus but larger, with a round belly like a spider and eight long tentacles. They are covered in thorns, similar to sea cucumbers, without scales or feet, resembling abalone. There is a type of seafood called "octopus fish" in Penglai, which is likely the same as the stonefish or another type of squid based on its appearance.

There is a sea snake, three feet long, stiff like a decayed rope, with a black color and a fierce appearance. Locals say it can kill insects, treat stubborn illnesses, and ward off plagues, perhaps similar to the Yizhe snake of Yongzhou! The local customs highly value it as a precious item.

There is a sea urchin resembling a hedgehog, with its meat removed, mashed into a paste, and stored in small bottles, suitable for drinking with alcohol.

There is a parasitic snail of varying sizes, with an elongated shape and a shell on its back, walking with legs. Inside the snail, there are crabs with two claws and eight legs, four large and four small, using the larger ones to walk and the smaller ones to hide. When touched, they retract their larger legs into their shells and use their larger claws to guard the entrance. The parasitic crabs also exhibit the traits of the parasitic snail, as mentioned in the "Haifu": "Crabs in the snail's belly," indicating a similar situation. It seems that there were crabs first, but when they were placed in a bowl with the parasitic snail, they struggled to escape. The result was too much force, causing the shell to fall off, and the crab immediately died, seemingly dependent on the snail's shell. The mysteries and wonders of nature are truly difficult to imagine.

There is a type of sand crab, broad but thin, with claws larger than its body. Its shell is small, with a piece missing in the front, but when the claws retract, it fits perfectly, seamless. Its eight legs are particularly short, and its abdomen lacks a shell, making it impossible to discern its gender. When it encounters people, its eyes sink in, and it spits out water over an inch high from its mouth, seemingly expressing anger. It can survive for more than ten days without food when kept in seawater.

There is a type of clam, over two feet in diameter and about five feet in circumference, known as "roof tile" because its shell's uneven shape resembles roofing tiles.

There is a type of seahorse meat, thinly sliced and curled like shavings, with a color resembling sliced Poria cocos. This is the most precious item, difficult to obtain, and once acquired, it is first offered to the king. Its appearance is like a fish body with a horse head, no fur but with legs, and its skin resembles that of a dolphin. These are specialties of Zhongshan Kingdom's seafood.

The fruits of this kingdom also have many varieties different from those in China. The fruit of the banana resembles fingers, golden yellow in color, sweet in taste, with segments resembling pomelo, also known as Ganluo. When it ripens, it turns green, but it becomes yellow when covered with sugar. Its flowers are red, with each flower spike several feet long. Every year, five or six fruit clusters are harvested, with one fruit produced per year per cluster. China also has bananas, but it is unheard of for them to fruit every year, or for banana fibers to be woven into cloth. Perhaps their nature is different.

The raw materials and methods of weaving cloth also differ from China. There is a type of cloth called banana cloth, beige in color and one foot wide, made by soaking banana fibers and then spinning them into cloth, soft and fine like silk.

There is a type of ramie cloth, pure white and delicate, one foot two inches wide, comparable to cotton cloth.

There is a type of silk cloth, pure white and soft, with ramie hemp as the warp and silk as the weft, the most precious fabric. The "Book of Han" mentions bananas, tubes, madder, and kudzu, referring to this type.

There is a type of hemp cloth, beige in color, but rough in texture, the lowest grade.

The people of Zhongshan are skilled in printing on cloth, using paper-cut patterns as samples. They place the paper-cut on the fabric, apply ash on top, remove the paper-cut after the ash dries, apply color to the blank areas, wash it in water after it dries, and the ash is washed away, revealing the colors. The more it's washed, the brighter the colors become, and even if the clothes are torn, the colors won't fade. There must be a special method of production, but the people of Zhongshan keep it a secret, so East Asian printed fabrics are highly valued by the people of southern Fujian.

The flowers, plants, and trees here mostly have different names from those in China. Unfortunately, I didn't bring the "Compendium of Flowers" with me, so I can't identify them one by one. The Cycad is called "Wood," the Holly is called "Fukumu," and the Chrysanthemum is called "Zenju." The Iron Tree is called "Fengweijiao," named after its leaves, which resemble phoenix tails, or "Seaside Palm," named after its palm-like top leaves. Some people bring it to China as a bonsai, calling it "Eternal Palm." The pineapple, when flowering, is called "male plant," with white petals resembling white lotus flowers, emitting a strong fragrance but not bearing fruit; the one that doesn't flower is called "female plant," but its fruit is large, edible like melons. Some say it's a variant of the breadfruit, while the people of Ryukyu call it "Ane." The Citron is called "Tenri Kō," with leaves resembling date trees, small white flowers, and very fragrant, with fruits resembling bamboo shoots but larger. It is said that in February, the bright red fruits cover the branches like burning flames, but unfortunately, I did not see them.

Ryukyu receives abundant sunlight and has a warm climate. It is already deep autumn, but the flowers and plants have not withered, the buzzing of mosquitoes and flies has not ceased, and the reeds are in full bloom. The wild peony blooms from March to August, with flowers hanging down like bells of various sizes, white petals with a faint purple blush on the edges, deep black flower hearts, round and large flowers, emitting a fragrant scent. The Bougainvillea blooms all year round, with white, deep red, and pink varieties. For this, I wrote a poem, which says: "Accompanying the envoy to the fairy isle, every day is filled with beauty. The weather is always like March or April, with flowers blooming continuously throughout the year."

The people of Ryukyu love orchids, calling them "Confucius flowers." In ancient mansions, there are particularly many precious varieties. There is a type of Wind Orchid, with leaves slightly longer than ordinary orchids, grown in bamboo baskets and hung in the wind to propagate. There is a type of Guardian Orchid, with leaves resembling cinnamon but thicker, initially shaped like fingers, one stem can produce eight or nine flowers, blooming in April, with a fragrance superior to ordinary orchids. It is named Guardian Orchid because it is produced between the rocks of Guardian Mountain, requiring no soil or water, some clinging to tree branches, some wrapped in palms hanging in the air, all thriving. There is a type of Su Orchid, also known as Zhi Orchid, with leaves resembling phoenix tails and flowers resembling pearls. There is a type of Stick Orchid, green in color, with stems resembling coral, no leaves, and flowers emerging from the branches like ordinary orchids, but smaller, also parasitic on trees. There are also flowers such as Ishigaki Pine Orchid and Bamboo Orchid, some brought from other islands, some obtained from between rocks, all with fragrances that are not inferior to ordinary orchids. For this, I composed a poem, which says: "Transplanting roots in a secluded isle, truly praiseworthy, said to be flourishing flowers in the heavens. Not comparable to ordinary grass and trees, flourishing as soon as the spring breeze arrives." After writing the poem, I also sketched the orchids, but I am ashamed that my brush is not as skilled as Huang Quan's when it comes to depicting flowers.

There are many floating stones along the coast, hollow inside, translucent and exquisite. When hit by seawater, they emit a sound like a bell, similar to the Stone Bell Mountain in Pengli Bay, China.

With nothing to do in my leisure time, I often play chess with Mr. Shi, using Ryukyu chess pieces. The white pieces are made from the sealed mouth of a sea snail, ground into stone. Small snails from the mainland have small round shells to protect their doorways, while large sea snails have shells that are up to five or six tenths thick, with a diameter of over two inches, round and white like chalcedony, called "seal stones" by the locals. The black pieces are made from blue stones. The diameter of the chess pieces is about six tenths, with a circumference of about two inches, concave in the middle and flat around the edges, with no distinction between the front and back, unlike Yunnan chess pieces. The chessboard is made of wooden boards, eight inches thick, with four legs, each four inches high, and the surface is engraved with chess lines. Playing chess is a local custom, with no hesitation in making moves, and there are also some national-level masters. After playing chess, the winner is determined by counting the number of empty eyes, regardless of whether there are actual pieces or not, and the results of the count are exactly the same. It is said that there is a chess god enshrined in the country, depicted as a heavenly maiden, rarely shown to others, showing the refined elegance of Zhongshan Kingdom.

On the eighth day of the sixth month, at eight o'clock in the morning, the envoys respectfully presented the imperial decree and conducted a sacrificial ceremony, offering incense and burning paper, placing the imperial decree in the Dragon Pavilion. Setting off from the Heavenly Embassy, they headed east, passing through Kumi Village and Poshan Village, and arrived at Anli Bridge (also known as Zhenyu Bridge). Shisun Wen followed the ceremonial etiquette to greet the envoys and then led them into the temple. After the ceremony, they were guided to visit the ancestral temple. The main temple has seven rooms, with a central opening leading to a shrine containing the ancestral tablets of all the kings of Zhongshan Kingdom: on the left, the tablets of sixteen kings from Shunma to Shangmu; on the right, the tablets of fifteen kings from Yiben to Shangjing.

On this day, the Ryukyu people who came to watch were everywhere. Men knelt by the roadside, while women gathered together to watch from a distance. Some set up curtains with bamboo curtains to watch, and locals said, "Those are the relatives of nobles and high officials." Women adorned their foreheads with black paint and their fingers with tooth sleeves as decoration. Those who applied more black paint turned completely black, while those who applied less left intervals painted with plum blossom patterns. The customs of Zhongshan Kingdom are such that they do not pierce their ears, apply powder, or wear jewelry and jade ornaments. At the entrance of every household, there are mostly "Stone Dares" steles erected, and the walls are mostly planted with Agave or bamboo trees, trimmed very neatly. The people of Zhongshan Kingdom refer to China as "Tangshan" and Chinese people as "Tangren."

The land of Ryukyu is all sandy soil, and once the rain stops, it becomes walkable without mud. There is a Qijin Pavilion on Mount Aoshan, where the envoy Chen Kan of the Ming Dynasty repelled the Jin troops when he returned, so the Ryukyu people built a pavilion to commemorate his merit. Bianyue is about three miles southeast of the royal palace. After passing through Yuanjue Temple, the water flows left and right from the ridge, which Feng Shui masters call "the passage," the Feng Shui lifeblood of Zhongshan Kingdom. There are five large and small peaks, with the highest one called Bianyue. The mountain is covered with dense shrubs, and there are two stone pillars in front of the mountain, with two fences in the middle and two wooden pavilions outside. Slightly to the left, there is a small stone pagoda, with five stone tables displayed on both sides. Turning east from here, dozens of steps lead to the mountaintop. There are two stone platforms on the top, one on the west for worshipping the mountain god and one on the east for worshipping the sea god. The sea god is called Zhu and is said to be the second daughter of Tian Sun. When the king accepts the enfeoffment, he must fast and personally offer sacrifices. In January, May, and September, sacrifices are made to the mountain god, the sea god, and the national guardian god, with the altar set up at Bianyue.

    I have already visited Poshi, Yukisaki, and Turtle Mountain, but overall, the scenery of Hetou is the most beautiful. I followed the chief and deputy envoys to visit Hetou Mountain, climbed to the top, and sat down to avoid the sun. I saw the grass blending into the sky, and the dense shade of pine and cypress covering the ground. Looking east towards the peak of Bianyue, one peak stands alone in mid-air, with the palace below vividly depicted. Looking south towards the mountain, I only saw calm seawater nearby, and distant mountain mists resembling embankments, with the towering Fengjian City standing tall and the former site of the Southern Palace faintly visible. Looking west at Ma Chi Mountain and Gumi Mountain, they appeared and disappeared intermittently, sometimes near, sometimes far, which is the route taken by the envoys. Looking down from the north at Naha and Kume, the bustling scene was prosperous. All the marvels of nature, the strange and wonderful high mountains and rivers, the shady and bright flowers, trees, and plants, the fluctuating movements of fish and birds, the changing clouds and mists, all displayed their wonders before my eyes. Only then did I realize how crude and simple my previous travels were.

    Doctor Liang prepared some wine and dishes simply, sitting on the ground, and I also had my servants bring some wine and dishes. At three in the afternoon, a cool breeze suddenly blew, and light rain was about to fall, so we packed up the dishes and boarded the boat. At this time, the tide was rising, and the seawater flooded the beach. We sailed along the south foot of Mount Aoshan and turned northeast. The mountain rocks on the cliffs by the shore stood precariously, and the seabirds flew like gulls, while fishing boats shuttled back and forth like weaving shuttles. Before long, the setting sun disappeared behind the mountain, and a bright moon leaped out of the sea, with countless colorful rays flying towards the tide. Zhao Jieshan and I raised our cups to admire the moon, rowing and singing loudly, drinking continuously, and the guests were all drunk. By the time we passed through Duli Village, it was already past midnight. In front of the Qijin Pavilion, neatly arranged torches illuminated the night as if it were daytime, and the people welcoming the envoys were all exhausted. So we returned together under the moonlight. This was the most enjoyable trip I had in Zhongshan Kingdom.

Below the Quanzhou Bridge is the lakeside. On clear nights, the twin arches hold a bright moon, and everything in the universe is clear and clear, like a glass world, which is one of Zhongshan's eight scenic spots. Wangquan, with its sweet water, is also one of Zhongshan's eight scenic spots. There is a pavilion inside the royal city where you can look out over the royal city, so we rested in the pavilion for a while, tasting the spring water from Ruiquan, and admiring the eight scenic spots of Zhongshan. The eight scenic spots of Zhongshan are: Quanzhou Moon Night, Seaside Tide Sound, Kume Bamboo Fence, Longdong Pine Waves, Sudden Cliff Sunset, Changhong Autumn Clearing, Chengyue Lingquan, and Zhongdao Banana Garden. There are many palm and purple bamboo trees under the pavilion, and the bamboo grows thickly, about three feet high, with narrow and long leaves resembling palm leaves. This is what is called Guanyin bamboo. Under the pavilion's south side, there are clam shells about eight feet long, filled with water for people to wash, and this is how I learned that large clams are hard to come by.

People in Zhongshan Kingdom do not use hot water for washing. Every household erects a stone post and places a stone basin or clam shell on top to store water, with a handled water container next to it. In the morning, they use the water container to scoop water for washing. Guests are also treated the same way. The ground here is mostly covered with grass, thin and soft like a carpet. When there is something important, fresh sand is used to cover it. The people of Zhongshan Kingdom take the shells of hawksbill turtles and make them into long hairpins, which are then brought to China by merchants from Fujian and Guangdong. The Ryukyu people do not know their value and think they are worthless. It's like near Kunlun Mountain, where people exchange magpies for jade, influenced by geographical environment.

On the top of Fengjian Mountain, there are the ruins of the former residence of the Southern King. Xu Baoguang's poem has the lines "The collapsed palace walls have no complete tiles; the desolate grass and livestock resemble a dilapidated village." The descendants of the Southern King, who now bear the surname Na, still gather and live here.

Tsuyama, pronounced as "Shizan" by the people of Zhongshan Kingdom. The characters in Ryukyu are phonetic, and there is no distinction in pronunciation between "ten" and "lost." It is suspected to be a misreading of the character "die." Vice Envoy Li Dingyuan compiled the pronunciation of Ryukyu as "Qiu Ya" and concluded that the rule is to read one character as two or three characters, or to read two or three characters as one character's sound, all based on semantics rather than pronunciation, which is called "sending messages," and all Ryukyu people know this. Sometimes more than one hundred characters or more than ten characters are read as one sound, which is completely different from Chinese pronunciation. Only those who are proficient in literature and knowledgeable in the country know how to read it, and ordinary people do not know.

The sons of officials and gentry families in Kume Village are taught to speak Chinese as soon as they learn to speak and to write Chinese characters as soon as they learn to write. At the age of ten, they are called "Ruoxiucai," and the king provides them with one stone of grain. At the age of fifteen, they shave their heads and receive a ceremony, first paying respects to Confucius and then to the king. The king records their names in the register and calls them "Xiucai," providing them with three stones of grain. After adulthood, they are selected as translators. The most prestigious figures in the cultural community of the country are the descendants of the thirty-six surnames of the Ming Dynasty. The people of Naha are engaged in business and mostly come from wealthy families. In the early years of the Ming Hongwu period, skilled sailors among the thirty-six surnames in Fujian were granted the privilege to travel between China and Ryukyu. The surnames Liang, Cai, Mao, Zheng, Chen, Zeng, Ruan, Jin, and others in Kume Village of Zhongshan Kingdom are all descendants of the thirty-six surnames and are still respected by the people.

Talking about profound theories and principles with the Ryukyu officials, there were many insights, so I sang and composed poetry with them. Law Minister Cai Wen, Grand Doctor Zijin Cheng Shunze, and Cai Wenbo, the three of them, have the air of poets in their poetry collections. Cheng Shunze also wrote the "Navigation

Guide," which describes sea travel in great detail. Cai Wen devoted himself to classical Chinese, with works such as "Suoweng's Sayings" and "Zhiyan," rooted in Confucianism and Daoism. Their scholarship is modeled after Zhu Xi, but they have not yet reached the level of mastery.

Most of Ryukyu's mountains are hard and barren, suitable only for growing sweet potatoes. The common people say that in the year of enfeoffment, it will definitely be a bumper harvest. There was a little drought in May this year, but fortunately, rain came as expected afterwards, and we finally had a great harvest, with sweet potatoes harvested four times. The people of Zhongshan Kingdom were doubly happy and said, "If it weren't for the enfeoffment year, there would never have been such a good harvest."

In early June, all the rice had been harvested. Ryukyu has abundant sunshine and a warm climate, so rice often matures early. It is planted in November and can be harvested in May and June. Sweet potatoes, on the other hand, can be planted all year round, with four harvests in a year being a good harvest and four harvests in a year being a bumper harvest. Ryukyu has few rice fields and many sweet potato fields. The common people make a living from sweet potatoes, while rice is only eaten by the royal family and officials. There are also wheat and beans, but the production is not high. On the twentieth day of May, the whole country worships the rice god, and if the worship is not conducted, even if the rice has been harvested and piled up in the granary, it is not dared to be taken home to eat.

In early July, the swallows were finally seen, but they did not build nests in the houses. Chinese swallows return in August, so the swallows here may not have been to China. They fly here in July and must have nests elsewhere. There is also another kind of seabird commonly known as the sea swallow, which is slightly larger than the purple swallow but has white feathers. Some are pure white like seagulls. Most of them build nests on the island, and some occasionally fly to China. People here consider them a symbol of good luck. There is a kind of tide bird, the male is pure black, the female is pure white, both have short legs and long tails, are tame, and do not avoid crowds. Xiangya bought a small dog, its fur pattern resembling a leopard, and its temperament alert and sensitive. It only eats sweet potatoes, indicating that the locals mostly eat sweet potatoes. There are many rats and sparrows in Ryukyu, especially the rats, which are rampant pests. There are also cats, but they do not catch rats, and the Ryukyu people treat them as pets. It can be seen that the temperament of animals will also change with the different geographical environments. There are very few eagles, geese, ducks, and geese here.

Pillows come in various shapes in Zhongshan Kingdom. Some are square like the "gui", some are circular with thin axles connecting them like wheels, and some have multiple layers of compartments like stationery boxes, all made of wood and finely crafted. Generally, they are three inches wide and five inches high, lacquered on the surface, some black and some red. When placed upright, they easily topple over when one turns over. According to the annotation of "Li Ji - Shao Yi", "ying" refers to an alert pillow. It is called "ying" because it is alert and enlightening. Additionally, during the Ming Dynasty, Ma Guang of the Wen Zheng Company made alert pillows from round wood. If one slept for a short while, the pillow would turn, waking the person up, prompting them to get up and study. These pillows in Zhongshan Kingdom are likely remnants of the alert pillow tradition.

In terms of clothing, the sewing always makes the garment front very wide, with sleeves two feet wide and no hem at the sleeve cuffs. The sleeves are especially short to facilitate work. Most garment fronts have no buttons or ties and are collectively called "qin". Men wear a large belt around their waist, with a standard length of one zhang and six chi, and a width of four cun. It is wrapped around the waist four or five times, with the remaining ends hanging between the hips. Items like tobacco pouches, paper bags, small knives, and combs are kept in the bosom, causing the garment front to appear wrinkled and protruding. Clothes without seams under the armpits are only worn by children and monks. Monks also wear short garments resembling vests, called "duan su" to indicate renunciation of secular life. This summarizes the general attire of the Ryukyu people.

Hats are made with thin wooden frames covered with folded handkerchiefs. There are seven layers in the front and eleven layers in the back. Hats made of floral brocade resemble traces left by leaking roofs from a distance and are the most precious in quality, worn only by the Regent King's uncles and prime ministers. The next tier is the flower purple hat worn by law enforcement officials. The next tier is the pure purple hat. Purple is considered the most prestigious color, followed by yellow, then red, with green and blue being less prestigious. Various fabrics are ranked with brocade being the most prestigious, followed by silk. Before being enfeoffed, the king wears a black gauze hat with double wings slanting upwards, adorned with gold thread and a crimson tassel hanging below the chin, tied with colorful silk threads underneath. When enfeoffed, the king wears a leather hat, shaped like the hats worn by actors portraying emperors in Chinese dramas, with seven petals arranged in the front. They wear dragon robes and jade belts around their waist.

Palanquins resemble Chinese pancake palanquins, with a large chair in the middle, covered by a large canopy. There are no curtains around, and the shafts are thick and long, without ropes or crossbars, carried by eight people, four on each side.

According to Du You's "Tong Dian", there is a custom in the Ryukyu Kingdom where women, after giving birth, must eat the placenta, roast themselves over fire to induce sweating. I asked Yang Wenfeng about this, and he replied, "Roasting over fire is indeed practiced, but eating the placenta is not." Nowadays, the custom of roasting over fire has been abandoned in Zhongshan Kingdom, with only Beishan still retaining some ancient customs.

Regarding marriage customs, they are very simple. Of course, prestigious families sometimes use fine wines, delicacies, and precious jewels as betrothal gifts. During weddings, they use local palanquins, decorate with lanterns and streamers, and play drums and gongs to welcome the bride. They do not fuss over dowries or bridal gifts, and parents immediately return home after sending their daughter to her husband's house. They do not entertain guests, only close relatives celebrate with wine, usually just a few people. "Sui Shu" says, "Ryukyu customs are such that when men and women are pleased with each other, they become a couple," which is an ancient custom passed down. I asked Zheng Degong about this, and he said, "When the thirty-six surnames first arrived, customs had not changed. Later, as they gradually learned about wedding etiquette, such customs were gradually abolished. Nowadays, if a married couple in the country commits adultery, they will be beheaded." It dawned on me then that Ryukyu's reputation as a country of etiquette is also due to the influence of the thirty-six surnames.

If common people have a funeral, neighbors gather to accompany the funeral, and onlookers also come to escort the coffin.

After burial, everyone returns home. If a prominent family has a funeral, close friends among colleagues also come to accompany the funeral procession. After the procession, they return without entertaining guests. Usually, monks write the nameplates for the deceased, writing "circumstances of great meditation" for men and "circumstances of meditation" for women; there is no term equivalent to "ancestor worship". Recently, officials also have their titles written. The coffin is three feet long, and the body can only be laid in it bent. Recently, officials have also used coffins five or six feet long, but commoners still follow the old customs.

People in this country have slightly shorter arms and elbows than the Chinese. "Zhao Ye Qian Zai" also says that Ryukyu people have short stature, resembling people from Kunlun. Most of the scholars and officials I've seen are indeed short in stature, but there are also those with long beards and full faces, those with tall and slender figures, and those who are corpulent with a waist circumference of ten units, indicating that previous descriptions may not be entirely reliable. Most people here have body odor, which ancient people called "yin di".

Families that have enjoyed royal salaries for generations bear surnames bestowed by the court. Most of the common knowledge class and ordinary people bear surnames derived from place names, without other names. Their descendants are referred to as "son of so-and-so" or "grandson of so-and-so", based on their surname. The terms "tian" and "mi" used here refer to surnames.

The military and legal system in Zhongshan Kingdom has only three chapters: those who kill receive the death penalty, those who injure or commit serious crimes are exiled, and those who commit minor crimes are punished by exposure to the scorching sun. Crime statistics are regularly compiled, and there have been no executions in the country for many years. Occasionally, there are those who commit capital crimes and choose to take their own lives by disembowelment.

On the night of the fifteenth day of the seventh month, I opened the window and saw two torches placed outside every household. I asked the locals about the reason, and they replied, "It is a custom in this country to hold a Bon festival on the fifteenth day of the seventh month, hoping to welcome the spirits. After the Bon festival, the torches are removed." The Bon festival is the equivalent of the "Yu Lan" festival in China. In recent days, I have seen children in the market holding paper flags, facing each other and waving, mimicking the appearance of welcoming spirits. This made me realize that the Bon festival in Zhongshan Kingdom is a custom for ancestor worship and a major ritual.

On the southern shore of Turtle Mountain, there is a lime cave where people in Zhongshan Kingdom burn shells of tortoises, large oysters, etc., to make lime. Lime powder made from burning is not as good as lime for whitewashing walls but has stronger adhesion than lime. Further northeast is a salt pond, where people in Zhongshan Kingdom boil salt.

On the twenty-fifth day of the seventh month, the ceremony of enfeoffment by the principal and deputy envoys is held, and the number of people watching along the way increases. The envoys ascend Mount Wansong and proceed eastward in a grand procession. The road is wide and well-maintained, passing through an archway with a plaque that reads "Zhongshan Road". Passing another archway, the plaque reads "Country of Etiquette". Prince Shangwen, wearing a leather hat and dragon robe, jade belt around his waist, dragging his skirts adorned with jade pendants, leads civil and military officials kneeling by the roadside to welcome them. Moving further, they reach the Gate of Joy, where the king's palace sits atop the mountain, built on stacked reef walls polished to resemble cliffs. There is a small path on the city walls, but no low walls, with heights exceeding five feet, making them appear to be constructed from stacked skulls from a distance. On the outer cliff of the city, the left side is engraved with the words "Longgang" and the right side with "Huzuo". The palace faces west because China is to the west across the sea, symbolizing loyalty and submission to China. Behind the palace faces east, there is the Jieshi Gate; to the left, facing south, is the Shuimen Gate, and to the right, facing north, is the Jiuqing Gate. Moving further inward, there is another layer of cliffs with a gate facing northwest called Ruiquan, with paths on both sides and doors on the left and right. Continuing, there is a sundial facing west with a plaque reading "Ke Lou", with a bronze pot dripping water to measure time. Further inside, there is another gate facing northwest called Feng Shen Gate, which is the main gate of the royal palace. The palace covers dozens of acres, with two roads paved inside leading to the inner courtyard, where the king handles state affairs. Hanging on the walls are paintings of Fuxi painting the eight trigrams, with a dragon and horse carrying the eight trigrams standing beside

King Wen. The colors of the painting are old and elegant, slightly worn, probably not a modern item. The palace in the north is sturdy and simple, with the roof easily reachable by hand, because it is located on a hill and needs to withstand hurricanes from the sea. Opposite the North Palace is the South Palace. On this day, the principal and deputy envoys host a grand banquet at the North Palace. The enfeoffment ceremony has been completed, and the country celebrates. It is said that wherever the king passes by, colorful decorations are arranged. On both sides of the road at Quanzaki Bridge, potted flowers and various exotic flowers are placed, surrounded by red railings. In the middle, there is a carved wooden kirin, with a plaque above reading "Neither dragon nor lion, neither bear nor tiger, auspicious beast of the king." In front of Tianfei Palace, six large pine trees are planted, four artificial hills are piled up, two white cranes are made, and there are three living deer, a mother and two fawns. A pavilion is erected over the pond, covered with pine branches hanging down like grapes. In the pond, there are five carved carps of various sizes, floating on the water. Surrounding the pond is a bamboo railing, next to which is a plaque called "Xie Le Fang". Hanging on the pillars of the plaque is a wooden board with the inscription "Lu Zhuo Zhuo, Niao He He, Ren Yu Yue." After returning, I told the deputy envoy about these, and he said, "These are all recorded in historical books. After several decades, not a single word has changed. It can truly be said to be an engraved text." All the accompanying guests laughed.

In Yomitan County, there was a man named Guishou who was extremely filial to his stepmother, a fact well known among the people. However, his stepmother favored her own biological son and would speak ill of Guishou in front of his father, Isa, even going as far as to refuse to eat in order to provoke Isa's anger. Deceived by her, Isa planned to kill Guishou and instructed him to fetch water from the northern palace late at night, intending to seize the opportunity to murder him. Guishou's servants hid him inside the house and went to advise Isa, but Isa tied up the servants before eventually releasing them. Realizing that his plan was exposed and reluctant to kill Guishou, Isa drove Guishou out of the house instead. Guishou, feeling despondent after being driven out, contemplated suicide but was concerned that doing so would expose his stepmother's wickedness. Just then, a hailstorm struck, and weakened by illness and exhaustion, Guishou collapsed on the road, frozen stiff. A patrol officer came across him, felt his body, and realizing he was still alive, covered him with his own clothes. Guishou gradually regained consciousness. As the officer questioned him, Guishou, unwilling to expose his stepmother's evil deeds, lied to him.

Initially, the patrol officer felt indignant upon hearing that Guishou was driven out of his home. Suspecting that the hesitant man before him was Guishou, the officer provided him with some food and clothing before letting him go, then secretly investigated to uncover Guishou's true situation. He then ordered the gathering of the entire village, where Isa's wife was brought to the meeting place, and her crimes were recounted before she was arrested and detained. Just as they were preparing to report to the king, Guishou offered to take the punishment in place of his stepmother. Moved by the filial son's heartfelt plea, the patrol officer decided not to harm Guishou and instead summoned Isa and his wife to reprimand them in person. Touched and enlightened by the woman's awakening, mother and son reconciled completely. The deputy envoy had already written a biography for Guishou, and I composed a poem to commend him further. The poem reads: "The sage in the carriage asks about customs in Qiu Yang, The hidden virtue must be brought to light. Genuine filial piety has always been recognized, No different from Min Sun and Wang Xiang." It serves as an admonishment to those who serve their stepmothers but fail to fulfill filial duty.

As we passed through Dianshan Township, it happened to be market day, so we strolled through the market. Most of the items bought and sold in the market were sweet potatoes, with some fish, salt, wine, vegetables, ceramics, wooden goods, banana fiber cloth, and coarse fabric, mostly of poor quality and not worth looking at. There are no specialized market shops in the country, and most people do their buying and selling at home. Items are exchanged using what one has for what one lacks, without the use of silver coins. I heard that the country uses Japanese Kan'ei coins, but I didn't see any during this visit. Yesterday, Xiangya showed me a string of coins, round like goose eyes, without sharp edges, strung together with string, accumulating to over three inches long when all four strings were combined, wrapped in paper and sealed with a special mark. These are the new coins made by the Ryukyu people, with each bundle equivalent to ten Chinese cash. Probably due to a shortage of coins in the country and the fear of others hoarding Kan'ei coins for themselves, they decided to produce these coins for circulation. As a result, there is no circulation of money in the market.

Men in Zhongshan Kingdom live leisurely lives, while women endure hardship, with no one carrying burdens on their shoulders. Women undertake tasks such as going to the market, spinning, sewing, fetching firewood, and carrying water, often balancing loads on their heads. Women's clothes have no buttons or ties, and they don't wear belts. Also, both men and women do not wear trousers, so they must hold their clothes with their hands. Women's clothes have longer fronts than men's, with the lower hem of the front folded into two layers, which prevents them from being blown open by the wind. This explains why women's hairpins must be skewed to one side, as their hands are already holding their clothes, leaving no room to carry things on their heads. They start practicing this skill from childhood, so even when carrying weights of a hundred catties, they can climb mountains and cross rivers without falling over. Women often roll up both sleeves to their backs and tie them with a rope when working. When their hair gets dirty, they wash it with mud to remove the dirt; they take off their clothes and tie them around their waist when washing, bare-chested, and don't avoid others when seen. They carry children with only one hand, resting them on their waist, using this to hold their clothes.

Dongyuan is located on Qishan, turning north after leaving the Huanhui Gate. Following the spring water flowing downstream from Ruiquan, we arrived at Longyuan Bridge, where the spring water converges into a pool about ten zhang wide and several dozen zhang long, protected by embankments, named "Longtan". The pool water is clear, and the fish are scarce, with half the lotus leaves. Turning east again, there is a small village with slender bamboo arranged like screens and tall and straight pine trees providing dense shade. Thin clouds drift through the forest, and a gentle breeze whistles through the bamboo. Outside Dongyuan Garden, there is already a tranquil charm.

Entering the garden gate, there are two plank pavilions facing south. Passing the pavilions and walking south, you'll see three houses. East of the pavilion, there is a small earthen mound, resembling an inverted basin. Turning south from here, there is a rock facing west, engraved with Sanskrit characters. Crouching beneath it is a stone lion, colorfully decorated. Moving further down, there is a small square pond with a stone-carved dragon head spouting water. There is also a goldfish pond, with dense bamboo groves to the front and a hundred green pines standing tall to the back. Continuing eastwards is the Wangxian Pavilion. In front, there is the "Dongyuan Pavilion", and behind, the "Nengren Hall". From the northeast, one can overlook the sea, and to the southwest, one can look up at the mountains. Renowned for its scenic beauty, Dongyuan ranks first among the attractions of Zhongshan Kingdom.

  The scenery of Nanyuan is no less splendid than Dongyuan. Passing through Zhongma and Fusheng, turning east, walking along the field path, one sees vast paddy fields of green sweet potatoes, showing no signs of autumn decay. Some of the sweet potatoes have just been planted, and upon inquiring, I learned that they have already been harvested three times. Advancing into the mountains, with pine shade lining the path and thatched cottages scattered about, the rural scenery is picturesque. After walking for more than ten li, we finally entered the village of Nanyuan, named Guchangchuan, which means "Gathering Joy Garden". Nanyuan sits atop the ridge, with five rooms arranged in a pavilion-like structure, intricately designed. In front of the pavilion is a newly excavated pond, elongated from east to west, with a few rocks piled on top as small bridges. To the south of the bridge, there is a newly built small hill, on which a pavilion has been built, suitable for gazing from the railing. To the east of the pavilion, some exotic flowers and plants have been planted. There is a flower that looks like a butterfly, deep red in color, with leaves resembling tender green locust leaves, called "Butterfly Flower"; there is also a type of pine leaf that looks like white hair, called "White Hair Pine". To the east of the pond, there used to be a bridge with a pavilion, but now it is replaced with a cloth painting. To the west of the pond, there is a loft, spacious and airy, suitable for cooling off in the breeze. There is also a loft named "Welcoming the Sun" and a pavilion named "Overlooking", both inscribed by the Chief and Deputy Envoys. To the north of the pavilion, there are pines, phoenix banana trees, peach trees, and willow trees. At dusk, smoke rises from the chimneys, much like in China.

  During our excursion to the sea with Jichen, we noticed that there were no other deities enshrined on the board pavilions, only banners made of copper plates inscribed with the words "Offered by the Imperial Coins", with the date "Second Year of Yuanhe, Renxu". Some people suspected it was from the Tang Dynasty, but it is not the case. According to research, the second year of Yuanhe (807 AD) was Dinghai, not Renxu. In "The Guide to the Eight Trigrams" written by Japanese Masamichi Norimasa, there is a chapter called "Three Elements Directive", which states: "The Upper Element starts from the seventh year of Yonglu and ends in the third year of Yuanhe; if the Element starts from the first year of Kwan'ei and ends in the third year of Yuanhe; the Lower Element starts from the first year of Zhengheng. Now it is the sixteenth year of Genroku, Bing Wei." Since Zhongshan Kingdom uses Japanese Kan'ei coins, using Yuanhe is a way for Ryukyu to use the title of the Empire to prove itself, indicating that Ryukyu once paid tribute to Japan, and today it is just a taboo not to mention it.

The making of kites is not very sophisticated, and most children stand on the roof to fly them. According to Chinese customs, kites are mostly flown before Qingming Festival because flying kites requires looking up with an open mouth, which can promote yang qi and help children stay healthy. Nowadays, Ryukyu people fly kites in September, not because kites cannot fly in September, but because the wind direction here is somewhat different from that in China. From this, it can be inferred that Ryukyu is sunny and warm, so rice can be planted in October.

According to the customs of Zhongshan Kingdom, if a man wishes to become a monk, his wish is respected. After receiving ordination, the state treasury provides him with living expenses. If he violates the precepts, he is ordered to return to secular life and exiled to another island. If a woman wishes to become a prostitute, her wish is also respected. The prostitute's brothers maintain their familial relationship with her clients, but they are all poor, so they do not feel ashamed. If a woman who is already married dares to commit adultery again, her father or brothers are allowed to kill her without reporting to the king, and even if they do report it, the king will not pardon her. This is the fundamental difference between the virtuous and the lowly in the country, and it is used to teach the people to value honor and shame.

There is a prostitute in red attire here with whom one cannot understand each other when speaking. Singing along to the rhythm, using dialects. But there is indeed a charm to it, almost comparable to Hang Garden. Recently, due to some urgent matters, I had to go to another place, and she asked me to write a poem for her while holding a fan, so I wrote two poems for her. The poems go:

At twenty-eight, she's most graceful and refined,
With a slender waist and captivating eyes so kind.
Holding her lute, she remains silent and coy,
Seeming familiar, as if met in Suzhou, oh boy.
With new sorrows and old regrets, emotions blend,
Meeting again, feels like worlds apart, my friend.
Sadly, tonight's moon shines bright and clear,
But with whom will she roll up the embroidered curtain to peer?

The people of Ryukyu Kingdom are very respectful and polite. Whenever they receive something, they always raise both hands to express their gratitude. When meeting someone they respect, they bow and then bow again after rubbing their hands together, then bow again. When persuading esteemed guests to drink, they hold the cup full of wine on their fingertips to show respect; for equals, they hold the cup in their palm.

The houses here are not tall and must be roofed with cylindrical tiles to prevent them from being blown away by hurricanes. The floor must be three feet above the ground to avoid dampness. The roof extends in all directions, resembling an octagonal pavilion. The houses are connected on all four sides without repeated structures or suites to save materials. There are no doors on the houses; instead, there are two grooves carved at the top, and square frames are installed with paper pasted on them. They slide left and right without bolts, which is convenient and saves trouble, relying on the absence of thieves. Houses facing the street are equipped with door bolts. The shrine is made of blue stones placed on the stove and filled with sand, used to worship ancestors and gods. Ryukyu Kingdom considers stones as gods, with no true gods passed down through tradition. Stone lions made of tiles are erected on the roofs, resembling the "beasts with horns and tails" described in the Sui Shu. The walls are not painted, indicating simplicity. Wealthy families may have painted walls or pasted flower letters, which is a sign of learning from Chinese customs and gradually becoming somewhat extravagant.

On Turtle Mountain stands a peak towering above, isolated from the surrounding mountains. Attached to the front is a small peak, about two zhang away from the main peak. The people of Zhongshan used stones to build a cave connecting the two peaks, about ten zhang high, with cloth curtains hanging on the east side. Without resting, we climbed up along the stone steps, passed through the cave, and climbed up more than ten levels of stone steps before reaching the summit. The summit is just big enough to accommodate a building, unnamed and spacious on all four sides, without windows. The Deputy Envoy said to me, "This building can overlook the entire Zhongshan Kingdom. It cannot be nameless." Therefore, he named it "Shu Tower" and wrote a postscript: "What does 'Shu' mean? It means alone. Why is the tower named 'Shu'? Because it stands alone on a solitary peak." Not mentioning 'alone' but 'Shu' because the Deputy Envoy is from Shu. The construction of this tower has reached a hundred years, but the Deputy Envoy has only just named it, as if waiting for future generations. To the left of the tower, one can overlook the green fields, to the right, one can lean on sturdy rocks, facing the sea in the back and directly facing Zhongshan in the front, sitting on the tower and looking into the distance, truly like being on a high building. I asked the Deputy Envoy again, "With a plaque, there must not be lacking couplets." The Deputy Envoy then wrote the four lines quoted above as a couplet. On the way back, walking along the coast to the west, the cliffs, caves, streams, and gullies are all peculiar and steep, another enjoyable journey.

Crossing Nan Mountain, passing through Siman Village, every household faces the sea, surrounded by strange rocks. Walking west along the coast, there is a mountain with verdant peaks thrusting into the air, with the veins of the mountain stretching into the sea. The mountain is called "Sand Peak." At this moment, the noon tide has just receded, and the white stones sparkle, with herds of horses galloping and splashing water like raindrops. Continuing westward, passing through Dalin Village, thickets grow into fences, and hundreds of fishing nets are hung on them. Outside the village, the rice fields stretch endlessly, with muddy ponds trapping the galloping hooves of horses, and herds of cattle grazing on the hills. The travel notes of Wang Jie said there are horses but no oxen, but it seems not entirely true.

People who speak Zhongshan dialect in the main island are given yellow hats by the government and appointed as chiefs. Every year, a "provincial envoy" (equivalent to an imperial commissioner) is sent to supervise and appease, called an executive officer, in charge of collecting taxes and handling lawsuits in the region, collecting local specialties from all over to present as tribute to the king. "Jianqie" is the title of officials from other provinces. Shuri, Tomari, Kume, and

Naha belong to the capital, so there are no provincial envoys, except for them, all other places have provincial envoys. Their duty is to get close to the common people, inspect the benefits and drawbacks of the jurisdiction, and then report them to the "provincial envoy." Jianqie is somewhat similar to the Chinese provincial governor. Zhongshan Kingdom has fourteen subordinate provinces, each with ten jianqie. There are twelve subordinate provinces in the Southern Mountain Province and nine in the Northern Mountain Province, with the same number of jianqie as subordinate provinces.

The customs of Zhongshan Kingdom, from the tenth to the fifteenth of the eighth lunar month, every household steams rice and mixes it with red beans as a gift to each other, to be enjoyed as a sacrifice to the moon. This custom is the same as in China. On the night of this day, the Deputy and Assistant Envoys invite their attendants to drink outdoors. The moonlight is clear as water, the sky is a deep blue, and there is not a breath of wind. The sound of the tide mixes with the sound of silk and bamboo instruments, drifting from afar. It feels as if one is in Penglai's Three Mountains, listening to Zijin playing the sheng and Magu playing the qin, cutting off all worldly ties at once, leaving the mind pure. In the vast universe, sharing the same bright moon. Recalling the past staying at Xiao Shuang Tower, the beautiful nights and scenes have all been gently passed by, now separated from Yunniang, can one not feel a myriad of emotions while facing the moon?

It is said that the eighteenth of the eighth lunar month is the birthday of the tides. The custom of Zhongshan Kingdom is to wait for the tides on the waves on this night. At midnight on this day, I came to the waves with Ji Chen. The grass was like a green carpet, softer with dew, and walking slowly with the help of servants, we sat down against the stone wall. At midnight, the tide finally arrived, like thousands of overlapping clouds rushing in with the sea. For a moment, the smell of the sea was particularly strong, as if there were sea monsters swirling in the sea breeze, and the golden snakes danced with lightning, the sky column seemed to be about to break, and the earth's axis was trembling faintly, the snow-like spray wetting our clothes, soaring up to a hundred feet high. There was no daring thought of peeping into the Dragon Palace, but it felt as if pushed by a mysterious force. In a trance, astonished by the mysterious and varied tides. Seeing this scene, one realizes that Mei Cheng's "Seven Lyrics" have not yet fully described it. After the tide receded, the sound of bells and drums came from between the reefs. We walked to Huguosi Temple, still feeling the thunderous tide reverberating in our ears. When the tide reaches this level, there is no need to see other tides.

From New Year's Day to the sixth day of the first lunar month, celebrate the Spring Festival. On the fifth day, respectfully welcome the Kitchen God. In February, worship the Wheat God. On the twelfth day, dredge the wells, draw fresh water, known as "washing away a hundred ailments." On the third day of the third lunar month, make artemisia cakes. On the fifth day of the fifth lunar month, hold dragon boat races. On the sixth day of the sixth lunar month, Zhongshan Kingdom celebrates the sixth month festival, with every household steaming glutinous rice as a gift to each other. On the eighth day of the twelfth lunar month, make glutinous rice cakes wrapped in bamboo leaves, steamed and gifted to each other, called "ghost cakes." On the twenty-fourth day, send off the Kitchen God. January, March, May, and September are auspicious months, and women enjoy themselves by the seaside, worshiping the water god and praying for happiness. On the first day of each month, everyone gathers to draw fresh water as an offering to the gods. This is just a rough overview of Ryukyu customs. I privately wonder that although the customs of Zhongshan Kingdom respect Buddhism, I do not know that the eighth day of the fourth lunar month is the birthday of the Buddha; and the "ghost cakes" on the eighth day of the twelfth lunar month resemble zongzi, but I do not know about the seven-treasure porridge.

The king gave us more than twenty pots of chrysanthemums, with lush foliage, and the names of the flowers were marked with bamboo sticks at the roots. Among them, three are particularly unique: one is called "Golden Brocade," with flowers in red, yellow, and white, small and numerous, shining like stars; one is called "Heavy Treasure," with petals resembling lotus flowers but smaller, in a light pink color; one is called "Plain Ball," with wider petals, unlike chrysanthemums, densely layered in thousands of layers, pure white like snow. They are all unseen before, and we composed a poem for them, which goes: "In Tao's fence and Han's garden, autumn colors abound, yet not necessarily did they have these flowers in their prime. Alas, your secluded beauty is truly regrettable, with no path to transplant you to the Central Plains."

I have seen the lion dance of Zhongshan Kingdom, made with

cloth for the lion's body, animal skin for the lion's head, silk threads for the lion's tail, colored silk cut into lion hair decorating the exterior, with the head, tail, mouth, and eyes all lifelike, then the eyes plated with gold, and teeth pasted with silver. Two people hide inside the lion, moving up and down, jumping and frolicking, portraying a lively and joyful appearance. I said, "This is akin to ancient entertainment." According to the "Music Treatise" in the Old Book of Tang, during the reign of Emperor Wu of Later Zhou, the Taiping music, also called "Five Direction Lion Dance," was created. Bai Juyi's "Western Liang Courtesan" writes: "Masked barbarians perform lion dance, carving wood for the head and threading silk for the tail. Gold-plated eyes and silver-pasted teeth, with swift movements in fur coats and lifted ears." It describes this lion dance.

Here, there is also a performance called "Stepping on Stilts." A horizontal beam is erected, about four feet high from the ground, and a wooden board one zhang and two chi long is placed on top, with both ends hanging freely to ensure balanced force. Two local women, dressed in colorful attire and equipped with silk scarves, stand facing each other and sing while looking at each other. Before the song is finished, they leap up and stand at the two ends of the wooden board. They start by gently squatting down and standing up, causing the board to move up and down like a water mill. Gradually, the movement becomes higher and higher. When the woman on the east side suddenly descends and strikes the board, the woman on the west side flies up over three zhang high, like a nimble swallow dancing in the air. Then the woman on the west side descends forcefully, and the woman on the east side flies up high again, resembling an eagle soaring into the sky. The movements alternate, the amplitude increases, the frequency accelerates, almost like a pheasant dancing in front of a mirror, no longer able to distinguish between shadow and reality. After a while, the momentum gradually subsides, the board gradually levels out, and when both ends of the board stabilize, the two women jump down together, their attire intact and standing steadily. Until the performance ends, not a single misstep is made, achieving such a level of skill is truly unprecedented.

The Ryukyu people are very straightforward in receiving and sending off guests, without the formalities of bowing and deference. When guests arrive, they are not greeted, but they sit down freely, and the host prepares a smoking rack, a stove, a bamboo tube, and a wooden box, placing the smoking pipe on the rack and filling the wooden box with tobacco leaves. If the guest is esteemed, tea is brewed for them, with a small amount of powder mixed with tea leaves, poured into half a cup of boiling water, and stirred with a small bamboo broom until the foam is level with the cup. When the guest leaves, there is no farewell. High-ranking officials often dip a bit of wine with chopsticks and offer it to the guest's lips as a sign of respect. Adding yellow sugar to sake is called "Fuku," and adding white sugar is called "Jiu," both are precious items for entertaining guests.

On the Double Ninth Festival, dragon boats are prepared for a competition at the Dragon Pond. The Ryukyu people also race dragon boats in May. The dragon boat race on the Double Ninth Festival is specifically set up to entertain envoys from the Heavenly Court. Therefore, I composed three poems to record the grand occasion at that time, which go:

Regretting the chrysanthemums neglected in the old homeland, I travel far away to a foreign land.

Watching dragon boat races at the Dragon Pond, mistaking the Double Ninth for the Duanwu Festival.

Last autumn in Dongting Bay, personally picking yellow flowers to adorn my hair.

Today, climbing high in a foreign land, gazing at the Husband Peak alone.

Awaiting the wind-carried news to return on a raft, just in time for early winter to reach home.

Having missed the chrysanthemum banquet before the frost, I still hope to visit the plum blossoms in the snow.

I heard that Cheng Shunze once bought fourteen characters of Su Shi's calligraphy from Tianjin, and now his descendants still treasure them as treasures. I wanted to borrow them for viewing but couldn't, so I went to see them in person. Upon opening the scroll, I saw vigorous strokes, like strange peaks and rocks, with a strong and inviolable demeanor, one can imagine the spirit of the Daoist scholar of that year. The characters have a diameter of over eight inches, and the content is: "Incense flies from the Hanlin, surrounding the rivers and wilds, spring reports from the South Bridge, gathering anew." There is a postscript, but no date. The calligraphy of Su Shi circulated in the world is treasured by everyone. Because Su Shi's achievement is great merit, and calligraphy is just a trivial matter he carried along, but it can also stand on its own, reaching such a realm. It can be seen that the skill of ancient scholars is truly boundless.

I also visited the ancestral hall of the Cai clan. The hall enshrines the portrait of Cai Junmo, and Cai Junmo's calligraphy was shown to us, confirming that it is indeed the direct lineage sect of Cai Junmo, who came to Ryukyu in the early Ming Dynasty and was one of the thirty-six surnames. The Cai clan can speak Chinese, and its members are elegant and charming. From the ancestral hall to his house, the flowers, trees, and plants all exude an elegant charm, the pond is as round as the moon, and I wrote a plaque for his residence, called "Moon Wave Mansion."

Most Ryukyu people are skilled in trimming trees and building artificial mountains, so literati families have artificial mountains for guests to visit. Long poles are erected in the courtyard, with small wooden boats set on top, each boat being two feet long, equipped with masts, rudders, sails, and oars. Five wind vanes are installed at both ends, with colored flags hung to test the wind direction. Families going out to sea often use it to predict the return date of their loved ones. When the south wind blows, the whole family rejoices, indicating that the person who went out to sea is coming back, and after the person returns from the sea, the colored flags are taken down. This is the legacy of ancient wind flags.

The king has a square inkstone, five inches long and two inches wide. There is a historical mine where a large inkstone is produced, one foot long and six inches wide, with the words "Made in the fourth year of Yongle" engraved on it, and on the back, the words "In the fourth month of the seventh year, Dongpo Jushi left it as a gift to Pan Bin" are engraved. It is known to be a gift from the previous Ming Dynasty emperor. In Zhongshan Kingdom, there is a collection of Su Shi's poems, which shows that the king of Zhongshan not only cherishes inkstones but also appreciates Su Shi's calligraphy.

Cotton paper and Qing paper are made from rice husks, with rough quality that is not suitable for writing. There are also wrapped paper, large ones of good quality, up to three feet long and about two feet wide, as white as jade, and small ones are half the size. There are also stamped poetry papers, which can be used as letters. In addition, there are surrounding screen papers, which are used for pasting on walls. Xu Baoguang wrote a poem about "Ball Paper": "Cold gold in hand, whiter than refined, the sides are like the sea waves, condensing into one piece. Kun knives cut straight in a diameter of one chi, layer upon layer like snowflakes without a face." It vividly describes it.

Between the Southern Cannon Tower, there are two stone tablets. One is inscribed with regular script, with slight erosion, and the three large characters "Made by decree" are clearly visible; the other is inscribed with the characters of Zhongshan Kingdom. The stone tablets were built in the twenty-first year of the Jiajing reign of the Ming Dynasty (1542 AD). However, I cannot recognize all the characters on it, but I can see that the brushwork is indeed vigorous and lively.

There is a tree called "Shanmi," also known as "Wild Hemp Maiden," whose leaves can be used as dye, and the seeds it produces resemble Chinese soapberry seeds, with a sour taste. The locals press it to make vinegar. The vinegar in Ryukyu is pure white in color, not very sour, and is used by consumers as rice vinegar, but with a different taste, perhaps made from Shanmi fruit.

At the banquet, guests all sat on the floor, with the east side considered the seat of honor, covered with felt. The food was served in small plates, each about one foot square, with two wooden boards as legs, about eight inches high. The dishes were served in four courses, not all at once. The first three courses were served with rice, and it wasn't until the fourth course that two pots of wine were served, with drinking limited to three rounds. Each dish was served one at a time, with the previous dish removed before the next one was served. The first dish served with rice was fried noodle cake, the second was fried rice flowers, and the third came with plain rice. Each time a dish or wine was served, the host personally lifted it and placed it in front of the guest, then bowed and retreated, rubbing their hands. Throughout the meal, the host did not dine with the guests, to show the utmost respect. This is the etiquette of entertaining distinguished guests in Ryukyu, where both guests and hosts are treated equally at the table. The dining customs of Ryukyu can be summarized as follows: dining is done seated on the floor, without tables or chairs, and the utensils resemble ancient food vessels. Even in wealthy households, dining consists only of a dish, rice, and a pair of chopsticks. Chopsticks are mostly made from fresh willow branches. The custom of wives not dining with the family still preserves the tradition of ancient times.

Behind the "Fumin Hall" in the Angel Embassy courtyard, there are two stone tablets left from ancient times. One lists the names of the enfeoffed Zhongshan kings and their envoys from the Ming Dynasty: in the fifth year of the Hongwu reign, Zhongshan King Chedu was enfeoffed, with envoy Tang Zai; in the second year of the Yongle reign, Wuning was enfeoffed, with envoy Shi Zhong; in the first year of the Hongxi reign, Bazi was enfeoffed, with envoy Chai Shan; in the seventh year of the Zhengtong reign, Shangzhong was enfeoffed, with envoys Yu Bian and Liu Xun; in the thirteenth year, Shang Sida was enfeoffed, with envoys Chen Chuan and Wan Xiang; in the second year of the Jingtai reign, Shang Jinfu was enfeoffed, with envoys Qiao Yi and Tong Shouhong; in the sixth year, Shang Taijiu was enfeoffed, with envoys Yan Cheng and Liu Jian; in the sixth year of the Tianshun reign, Shangde was enfeoffed, with envoys Pan Rong and Cai Zhe; in the sixth year of the Chenghua reign, Shang Yuan was enfeoffed, with envoys Guan Rong and Han Wen; in the thirteenth year, Shang Zhen was enfeoffed, with envoys Dong Min and Zhang Xiang; in the seventh year of the Jiajing reign, Shang Qing was enfeoffed, with envoys Chen Kan and Gao Cheng; in the forty-first year, Shang Yuan was enfeoffed, with envoys Guo Rulin and Li Jichun; in the fourth year of the Wanli reign, Shang Yong was enfeoffed, with envoys Xiao Chongye and Xie Jie; in the twenty-ninth year, Shang Ning was enfeoffed, with envoys Xia Ziyang and Wang Shizheng; in the first year of the Chongzhen reign, Shang Feng was enfeoffed, with envoys Du Sance and Yang Lun. A total of fifteen times, twenty-seven people. Before Chai Shan, there were no deputy envoys. The other tablet lists the names of the Zhongshan kings and their envoys from the present dynasty: in the second year of the Kangxi reign, Shang Zhi was enfeoffed, with envoys Zhang Xueli and Wang Gai; in the twenty-first year, Shang Zhen was enfeoffed, with envoys Wang Ji and Lin Lin; in the fifty-eighth year, Shang Jing was enfeoffed, with envoys Hai Bao and Xu Baoguang; in the twenty-first year of the Qianlong reign, Shang Mu was enfeoffed, with envoys Quan Kui and Zhou Huang. A total of four times, eight people.

After Qingming, there is often a south wind blowing; after Frost's Descent, there are often north and south winds blowing. Violating this rule may lead to the onset of a hurricane. Hurricanes mostly occur in January, February, and March, while winds are prevalent in May, June, July, and August. Hurricanes come suddenly but leave quickly, while winds gradually escalate but last for several days. In September, there are sometimes north winds for a whole month, known as the "nine descending winds." Occasionally, there may be winds like hurricanes, coming and going abruptly. It is bearable to encounter hurricanes, but difficult to withstand winds. After October, there are mostly north winds, and hurricanes and winds come unexpectedly. Boatmen navigate the sea during the intervals between hurricanes and winds. When a hurricane is about to occur, there are black spots in the sky, and sailors must quickly take down the sails and prepare the rudder, any hesitation may be too late, and even lead to capsizing. Just before a hurricane, there are intermittent rainbows in the sky, resembling sails, called "broken sails"; after a while, they cover half the sky, resembling the tails of mantis shrimps, called "bent mantis shrimps." If these signs appear in the north, the storm will be particularly violent. Additionally, if the sea suddenly changes, with many dirty things like rice bran appearing on the surface, sea snakes swimming, or red dragonflies hovering, it is a sign that a hurricane is imminent.

  Since arriving in Ryukyu, half a year has passed in the blink of an eye, with no east wind to return home. On the twenty-fifth of October, we finally set sail back to our country. By the twenty-ninth, we saw Nanqishan in Wenzhou. Soon after, we saw Beiqishan, with dozens of ships anchored there. The people on board were very happy, thinking that they were the ships coming to escort them. The lookout on the stern boarded the ship and reported in amazement, "The anchored ships are pirate ships." He further reported, "All the pirate ships have raised their sails." Soon, sixteen pirate ships came roaring towards us. Our ship fired the stern guns, immediately killing four people, and those who were shouting were hit and fell into the sea, causing the pirates to retreat. Our guns fired again, killing six more people, then with cannon fire, five more were killed. Gradually advancing, we fired again, killing four more, and the pirates finally retreated. At this point, the pirate ships were upwind, so we quietly moved the guns to the starboard side of the helm, firing repeatedly to kill twelve pirates, causing the lead pirate ship's sails to catch fire, and all the pirate ships turned back. Among them, two pirate ships were larger and more boisterous, sailing downwind. Our cannons targeted them, and with a single shot, the lead pirate ship was hit, and smoke filled the air. When the smoke cleared, all the pirate ships had already retreated. In this battle, our guns were accurate, and we narrowly escaped disaster.

    In less than an hour, a north wind blew again, with waves splashing over the bow of the ship. In my sleep, I heard the people on the ship shouting loudly, "We've reached Guantang!" I was awakened. The companions hadn't slept all night and said to me, "With such danger, how can you still sleep?" I inquired about the situation at the time, and they said, "Each time the ship capsized, the sails lay flat on the water, and when a big wave passed over the bow, the ship would sink into the water, with the sound of rushing water non-stop. It's fortunate that the ship didn't capsize!" I smiled and replied, "If the ship had capsized, would you have been spared? I entered into sweet darkness without witnessing the danger at the time, isn't that lucky?" After washing up, I climbed onto the platform to observe and saw that more than ten stoves in front and back were gone, and there was nothing on the ship's surface, the cooking fire had long been extinguished. The boatman pointed ahead and said, "We're approaching Dinghai, no need to worry anymore." At six o'clock in the afternoon, the ship finally docked ashore. The boatman went ashore to buy rice and firewood, and we finally had a meal.

    That night, I wrote a letter to my family, to comfort Yun's longing and worry, but my desire to return home became even more urgent. I still remember, Yun once said to me, "Wearing simple clothes, eating simple meals, one can be happy for a lifetime, there's no need to travel far." This voyage, although filled with adventures and dangers, we narrowly escaped every time, but I have come to deeply understand Yun's words.

VOLUME SIX: THE WAY TO HEALTH

Since Yun's passing, I have been melancholic all day long. Every sunrise and sunset, every mountain and water excursion, is filled with scenes that sadden the heart. Reading "Records of Hardships and Sorrows," one can understand the extent of my difficulties and misfortunes.

In contemplating methods of liberation, I prepared to leave home and seek a life beyond the mundane world, in pursuit of an immortal existence. Later, due to the persuasion of brothers Xia Dan'an and Xia Yishan, I temporarily took refuge in the neighboring Zen temple, finding solace in the "Book of Zhuangzi." It was then that I learned of Zhuangzi's wife's death, and his response of drumming on a basin and singing. This was not a true state of forgetfulness; it was simply resignation to fate! As I delved into Zhuangzi's writings, I gradually gained some insight.

Reading "On Nourishing Life," I realized that for those who maintain an optimistic outlook, there is never a time without peace, nor a situation too challenging to endure. It's as if they are in harmony with the creator. What then is there to gain or lose, to live or die? Thus, all experiences are allowed to unfold naturally, and both sorrow and joy cease to exist within the heart. Reading "The Idle Excursion," I grasped the essence of nurturing life: it lies in leisure and freedom from worldly constraints, in finding contentment and pleasure in oneself. This made me regret my past infatuation; was it not akin to binding oneself in a cocoon?

This is why I write "The Way to Health." I also incorporate the teachings of past sages, seeking to alleviate various troubles and focusing primarily on benefiting the body and mind, in line with Zhuangzi's teachings. Perhaps, through this, one can preserve life and enjoy a full lifespan.

Though I am only forty years old, signs of aging have begun to appear. This is due to the various worries that have afflicted my body and mind over the years, the prolonged depression and suppression of emotions, which undoubtedly harm one's health. Xia Dan'an advised me to sit quietly every day, following the methods described in Su Shi's "Song of Nurturing Life." I intend to do just that.

The method of regulating the breath is not bound by time. Sit upright, like a puppet, loosen your clothes and belt to ensure comfort. Move your tongue in your mouth several times, slowly exhale without making a sound, then slowly inhale through the nose. Sometimes fifteen times, sometimes fourteen. Swallow saliva when it accumulates, then gently tap your upper and lower teeth together. Place the tip of your tongue against the roof of your mouth, slightly touching your lips to your teeth, and half-close your eyes to make your vision hazy. Gradually adjust your breathing to be even and fine, neither panting nor coarse. Count the exhalations or inhalations from one to ten, from ten to a hundred, focusing your attention solely on counting, without distraction. This is the state of "silence, stillness, and emptiness" described by Su Shi. If the mind and breath become unified, free from distractions, stop counting and let it flow naturally. This is what Su Shi calls "follow." The longer you sit, the better the effect. If you wish to stand up, do so slowly and gently, without sudden movements. With consistent practice, one may enter a state of meditation and experience various extraordinary phenomena. This is what Su Shi refers to as "attaining wisdom." In this way, clarity and enlightenment naturally arise, as if a blind person suddenly gained sight, truly understanding the nature of the mind, not just for the sake of maintaining the body or preserving life.

Exhale and inhale continuously, subtly and imperceptibly, with the spirit and breath mutually dependent. This is true breath. Each breath can be traced back to its root, naturally aligning with the laws of nature. This is the marvelous path to immortality.

While others speak loudly, I speak softly; while others worry much, I worry little; while others anger and fear, I remain calm. Tranquil and nonchalant, with a contented and fulfilled demeanor, this is the elixir of longevity. As Ouyang Xiu said in "Autumn Sounds," worrying about matters beyond one's control will turn a rosy complexion into withered wood and black hair into streaks of white. This is a common affliction among scholars. Furthermore, he said, "Countless worries unsettle the mind, and myriad concerns wear down the body. When the mind is agitated, it will undoubtedly disturb the spirit." If one frequently succumbs to excessive worries and thoughts, then aging will accelerate in one's prime, leading to rapid decline in old age. Conversely, this is the method of longevity. Dancing with long sleeves and singing with feather fans, in the blink of an eye, everything changes; beauties and music in brothels are but fleeting illusions. Illuminated by the candle of spiritual nature, cutting off the desires of infatuation with the sword of wisdom, this is not something achievable by the faint of heart. However, emotions must find expression; it is better to place them in flowers, trees, and paintings than to be enslaved by glamorous beauties. This can alleviate many troubles.

Fan Zhongyan once said, "Even the wisest cannot avoid birth and death, nor can they control matters after death. Alone, we emerge from nothingness, yet must return to nothingness. Who is close, who is distant? Who can truly control all things? Since helplessness is inevitable, one should let go of ambitions, be carefree, and allow things to come and go freely. By severing worries and disturbances, one can gradually calm the mind, harmonize the five viscera, and only then will medicine have effect, and food have flavor. Like those who are at peace and joyous, there are no worries in their hearts. If the heart is troubled, one will lose their appetite; furthermore, when plagued by illness for a long time, one must worry about dying, and even worry about what happens after death, living in tremendous fear, how can one eat and drink? Please, relax and focus on nurturing life." This is a letter from Fan Zhongyan, advising his third brother to let go. In my recent days of worry and anxiety, it is fitting to read these words.

Lu You's mind is broad and vast, akin to Tao Yuanming, Bai Juyi, Shao Yong, Su Shi, and others, displaying a lofty and elegant demeanor. He has profound insights into the path of nurturing life and can truly be called a virtuous man. In the future, I intend to frequently study and ponder Lu You's poetry; it can serve as a remedy for my ailment.

Bathing is extremely beneficial. I recently made a large bathtub that can hold a lot of water. After bathing, one feels incredibly refreshed and comfortable. As Su Dongpo said in his poetry, "The basin overflows, the river pours, originally without impurities, washing makes it lighter." I have already experienced some of the subtleties within.

Treating illness after it occurs is not as effective as nurturing oneself when healthy. Treating the body is not as effective as treating the mind. Allowing others to treat oneself is not as effective as treating oneself first. Lin Jiantang's poem says, "One's own heart disease, one's own knowledge, thinking should be treated. Only when the heart creates illness, how can there be illness?" This is the prescription for self-treatment. Let the mind wander in emptiness, let the spirit concentrate in subtlety, dissolve worries in a state of desirelessness, and return the meaning of life to a state of non-action, thus achieving profound insight into life and prolonging one's life, eternally accompanied by the Tao.

"The Immortal Classic" considers essence, energy, and spirit as the inner three treasures, and ears, eyes, and mouth as the outer three treasures. It constantly admonishes the inner three treasures not to pursue worldly desires and leak outwardly, and the outer three treasures not to induce worries in the mind. Master Chong Yang advised to keep the mind as stable as Mount Tai in all twelve daily periods, whether walking, sitting, or lying down, without wavering. Vigilantly guard the gateways of the eyes, ears, nose, and mouth, not allowing evil energy to enter and true energy to exit. This is called "nurturing life is crucial." Without external exertion on the body and without brooding over worries, prioritizing tranquility and joy in life, and achieving a state of contentment, this is the realm of cultivation. Thus, the body will not tire, and the spirit will not dissipate.

The elderly of Yizhou once said: "Anyone who wishes for a healthy body must first correct their mindset. Achieving a state where the mind does not recklessly seek, does not cling to fantasies, does not crave desires and pleasures, and is not confused by temptations will naturally bring tranquility to the spirit. With a tranquil spirit, even if the limbs and hundred bones are afflicted with illness, they will not be difficult to treat. But if this spirit wavers, it will invite a hundred ailments, and even if Bian Que or Hua Tuo were by your side, they would have no way to treat you."

Mr. Lin Jiantang has six poems titled "Lu'an Poetry," which are truly the key to longevity. The poems say:
    I possess a small pill of elixir,
    Capable of curing the ailments of all.
    Once ingested, the body is at peace,
    Guaranteeing longevity and extending life.
    Understanding the heart method, who knows?
    Using invisible miraculous medicine to heal.
    By healing this heart, one can avoid illness,
    And leap into the realm of the Great Void.

Thoughts arise from various karmic sources,
Chaotic and disturbing, how to resolve?
There is a profound and mysterious method to dispel demons,
Guiding one into the peaceful abode of Yao and Shun.
Man possesses dual minds to reveal thoughts,
Only when there are no dual minds can one be truly human.
When the human mind is without duality, free from thoughts,
Thoughts extinguished, one sees the utmost clarity.
This and that, all fades away,
Turmoil and confusion give way to understanding.
With clouds parting, a clear light shines for thousands of miles,
The bright moon rounds and shines brightly.
Traveling the four seas to cultivate magnanimity,
The heart connects with the azure waters, waters connect with the sky.
At the river's edge, there's a fisherman to ask,
In the cave, peach blossoms bloom fresh every day.

A Zen master once discussed with me the method of nurturing the mind, saying: "The mind is like a clear mirror, do not let it gather dust; the mind is like still water, do not let it stir up waves." This statement aligns perfectly with what Zhu Xi said: "Scholars must always remind themselves to keep their minds alert and not fall into slumber, like the sun at its zenith, all evils will naturally cease." He also said: "Do not look with wandering eyes, do not listen with wandering ears, do not speak with wandering mouth, do not move with wandering mind, let go of greed, anger, delusion, and attachment, let go of right and wrong, self and others, let everything go. There is no need to predict what has not yet happened, do not overly worry about things that happen, do not dwell on past events, let things happen naturally, respond naturally, trust that they will pass naturally. Then, anger, fear, joy, and sorrow will each find their place." This is the key to nurturing the mind and will.

Wang Huazi said: "Fasting means to be moderate. To be moderate in spirit, to be pure in body, is not just about eating vegetarian food. To be moderate in spirit means to be indifferent to emotions, not to seek advancement, to disregard gains and losses, to be diligent in introspection, and to stay away from meat, fish, and wine; to be pure in body means not to walk crooked paths, not to look at ugly colors, not to listen to obscene sounds, not to be tempted by desires. Enter the room, close the door, light incense, sit quietly, this is true fasting. If one can indeed do this, then the divine within the body will be at peace, rising and falling unhindered, able to eliminate diseases, and live long without aging."

My living space has windows on all four sides, closed when there is wind, opened when it stops. In front of me, there are curtains, behind me, a screen. If it's too bright, I lower the curtains to soften the light in the room; if it's too dark, I roll up the curtains to let in the outside light. Internally, to keep the mind stable, externally, to keep the eyes comfortable, with both mind and eyes at ease, the whole body is also at ease."

The Zen master told me two verses: "Learn death before dying; kill life while alive." Being alive means that evil thoughts have just arisen; killing life means immediately eradicating them. This is similar to the function of "do not forget, do not assist" in Mencius.

Master Sun's "Health Song" says:
Health depends on knowing three prohibitions,
Great anger, great desire, and great intoxication.
If any of these still linger,
Beware of depleting true vital energy.
It also says:
People want to know the way of health,
Happiness and joy should be constant, anger and anger should be few.
With a sincere heart and proper intention, thoughts should be eliminated,
Reasoning should be straightened, the body should be cultivated to eliminate troubles.
It also says:
Forcibly drinking after drunkenness, full meals after gluttony,
There has never been a life without illness.
Eat and drink to nourish the body,
But avoid excess to maintain comfort.
It also says:
Don't let wine intoxicate you, it harms the spirit and damages the mind.
Drinking water when thirsty and sipping tea,
From the waist down, one will feel light.
It also says:
Seeing, hearing, walking, and sitting should not be prolonged,
The five exertions and seven injuries will result.

The limbs also need a little exertion,
Like a hinge, it will not rot.
It also says:
Daoists have their own principles for health,
Firstly, people should have little anger.
If these health songs can indeed be followed and practiced, and morning and evening exercises are maintained, they will show results. Don't think of them as cliches.

Clean up a room, open windows to the south, with eight windows bright and clear. Do not display too many antiques and curios to avoid disturbing people's minds and eyes. Place a large bed, a long table, pens, inkstones neatly arranged, with a small table on the side, hang a painting, and change it frequently. Place one or two books on the table, a piece of calligraphy, and a guqin. Keep the mind and body pure between the heart and form.

In the morning, enter the garden, plant vegetables, fruits, weed, water flowers, and plant herbs. When you come back indoors, close your eyes and rest your spirit. Sometimes read enjoyable books to make the spirit happy and content. Sometimes chant good poetry to express your sentiments. Stand before ancient calligraphy, play the ancient qin, and stop when tired. Gather with trusted friends for casual conversations, avoiding discussions of current affairs or power struggles, refraining from praising or criticizing others, and not arguing right or wrong. Occasionally, make plans to travel with companions, dress casually, and do not exhaust yourself with formalities. Have a little wine, but do not get drunk; being relaxed and happy is enough. If one can truly do this, it can be considered a joyful state of mind. From this, it can be seen that those who are entangled in snares, entrapped by worldly affairs, and burdened by official duties are indeed worlds apart from those who cultivate joy and preserve their spirits.

Tai Chi Chuan cannot be compared to other martial arts. The two characters of Tai Chi already completely encompass the meaning of this martial art. Tai Chi is a circle, and Tai Chi Chuan is a martial art composed of countless interconnected circles. Whether raising a hand or stepping, one must not depart from this circle; if one does, it violates the principles of Tai Chi Chuan. When the limbs and hundred bones are still, it's fine, but once movement starts, none can deviate from this circle, always becoming circular, sometimes empty and sometimes full. Before practicing Tai Chi Chuan, one must first concentrate and take a deep breath, sitting quietly for a moment, but this is not a Daoist technique. Just stop thinking, making sure to calm all kinds of distracting thoughts. When practicing, the principle is slowness, the key is to exert no force, continuous from beginning to end. It is said that Zhang Tong from Liaoyang, summoned to the capital in the early Ming Dynasty, encountered obstacles at Wudang, and dreamed of a stranger teaching him this martial art at night. In recent years, I have begun to adhere to the practice, and indeed feel that my body is relatively strong, impervious to severe cold or heat, and beneficial for physical fitness, with only advantages and no disadvantages.

Speak less, exchange fewer letters, socialize less, fantasize less, but as long as there is still breath, what is indispensable is accumulating virtue and nurturing the heart.

Yang Lianfu has a poem titled "Encountering Three Old Men," which says:

In front of the old man, present your words, embracing the whole of the Great Dao.

In front of the middle-aged man, present your words, announcing the seasons of cold and heat.

In front of the old man, present your words, who has slept half a century.

There was also a poem in the "Houshan Poetry" with the same meaning. They all originated from the poem of Ying Qu:

There was once a traveler on the road, who encountered three old men.

Each was over a hundred years old, working together to hoe the fields.

Going forward, he asked the three old men, how they achieved such longevity?

In front of the old man, present your words, his dwelling was crude and plain.

In front of the middle-aged man, present your words, he controlled his food and restrained his desires.

In front of the old man, present your words, he never covered his head when sleeping at night.

Indeed, the words of the three old men, that's how they could live so long.

The ancients said: "Compared to those above, we are lacking; compared to those below, we have more." This is the most wonderful way to seek happiness. Compared to those who cry due to hunger, we should feel happy if we can eat our fill; compared to those who shiver from cold, we should feel happy if we can dress warmly; compared to those toiling in service, we should feel happy if we can enjoy leisure; compared to those afflicted with illness, we should feel happy if we have good health; compared to those facing disasters, we should feel happy if we are safe and sound; compared to those who have passed away, we should feel happy to be alive.

Bai Juyi had a poem that goes:
What's the point of arguing within the snail's shell,
When my spirit can roam freely in the light of fire and stone?
In prosperity or adversity, let's rejoice,
To not laugh is folly indeed.
A contemporary poet wrote:
Life in this world is but a big dream,
Why take it so seriously and suffer in earnest?
Short or long, they're all just dreams,
Suddenly waking up, where does the dream go?
This is similar to Bai Juyi's broad-mindedness!

"The world is vast, time is limited, why bother toil and rush? Life is mundane and arduous, arguing about superiority and inferiority, length and shortness, but failing to realize that all things have their fate, gains and losses are difficult to estimate. Look at the desolation of the Jin Valley, the bleakness of the Wu River, the desolation of the Afang Palace, the wilderness of the Bronze Sparrow Terrace; glory and wealth are like dew on flowers, prosperity is like frost on grass. Seeing through a thousand schemes, casting aside ten thousand thoughts; why boast about dragon towers and phoenix halls, talking about what chains of profit and fame, grasping leisure and tranquility to live one's days, indulging in poetry and wine with abandon; singing 'It's not too late to return,' chanting 'The lake and sea are vast.' Enjoying the auspicious time and beautiful scenery, picking and arranging green leaves, searching for fragrant flowers, making arrangements with close friends, going to the riverside in the wild, sometimes playing the qin and chess to enjoy oneself, sometimes toasting and exchanging cups as the water flows; sometimes discussing the causes and effects of good and evil, sometimes discussing the rise and fall of the past and present; seeing flowers bloom like embroidered silk on branches, listening to birds sing like playing flutes. Letting go of the warmth and coldness of human feelings, the world's vicissitudes, wandering leisurely through the years, carefree through the passing of time." I don't know who composed this tune. After reading it, it's like waking up from a big dream, pasting a cool breeze on the bustling world.

Master Cheng Hao said: "I inherited a thin innate qi, so I pay special attention to nurturing life. By thirty, I gradually became strong, even stronger at forty and fifty, and perfected after fifty. I am now seventy-two years old, and as for my muscles and bones, they are undamaged compared to my prime. If one waits until old age to nurture life, it is like starting to save money after becoming poor. Even if one is very diligent, it will be of no avail."

Speak less, have fewer concerns, eat less. With these "three lesses," one can live long and ageless like a deity.

Drinking alcohol should be done in moderation, anger should be quickly dispelled, desires should be diligently controlled. Following these "three shoulds," illnesses will naturally be fewer.

There are ten methods for preventing diseases: 1. Observe the world in silence, understand that the basis of the "four elements" is based on false ideas; 2. When troubles arise, compare them with death; 3. Often compare oneself with those less fortunate, skillfully self-relieving; 4. The Creator makes us work hard throughout our lives, and only when we are ill do we have some leisure, so we should feel fortunate; 5. If past grievances come to light, accept them joyfully as they cannot be avoided; 6. A harmonious family, with no quarrels; 7. Everyone has their own reasons for illness, so self-observation and preventive treatment should be practiced often; 8. Be cautious of wind and cold, and make desires light; 9. Control food intake, maintain comfortable living conditions without overexertion; 10. Find wise friends to discuss happy, otherworldly topics.

Shao Kangjie lived in a peaceful abode and sang to himself:
In old age, limbs crave warmth,
In the peaceful abode, there's a hint of spring.
With all worldly matters off my mind, reclining,
I freely extend my limbs as I please.
In the heat, the bamboo brings coolness,
In the cold, a fire warms the blankets.
During the day, the falling petals and bird songs,
At night, inviting the bright moon to accompany the qin.
Regarding food, moderation is always considered,
Regarding clothing, warmth should not be neglected.

Who says the old are clumsy in their ways,
Yet they can still nourish their own bodies.

The way to nurturing life lies in the four words "pure and clear." Internally, feel that one's body and mind are empty; externally, perceive the world and external things as empty; break all kinds of delusions and attachments, without any insistence, this is called "pure and clear."

All the toxins of diseases arise from "density" (strong desires). Being dense in music and dance leads to weakness and cowardice; being dense in material interests leads to gluttony; being dense in fame and career leads to affectation. Being dense in reputation and honor leads to affectation and resentment. Alas, "density" is a highly toxic thing. Mr. Fan Shangmo uses a single remedy, called "dilution." The clouds drift lightly, the mountains are verdant, the stream murmurs, the rocks stand tall, the flowers sway in the spring breeze, the birds sing, the woodcutter sings, and the valley echoes. The vast world is originally peaceful and leisurely; it is the human heart that creates the noise.

At the end of the year, I visited Xia Dan'an and saw that his room was filled with dust, but he didn't mind. I sighed and said, "The place you live in must be cleaned thoroughly. Living in a quiet room, free from any dust and noise, is refreshing. Plant some flowers and trees in front of your house, and observe their growth regularly. Sit alone in the late night, occasionally open the window to let the moonlight in, it's especially refreshing. One feels as if the clear air from afar is flowing freely between heaven and earth, with the heart and clear air flowing unimpeded, without any blockages. Now, your living space is messy and dirty, not cleaning it up, don't think it's troublesome, a messy environment may not necessarily be helpful for a refreshing demeanor."

In recent years, I have been living calmly in a dilapidated temple, quickly shedding my past bad habits. Sometimes, I sing loudly in the woods, sometimes I howl alone in the quiet mountain valleys, sometimes I fish in the stream by boat. Abandoning desires and thoughts, over time, it seems that there have been some gains.

Chen Baisha said: "Not burdened by external things, not burdened by sounds and beauty, not burdened by haste and confusion, like eagles soaring high, like fish swimming freely, the key lies within me." Understanding this principle can be considered as being good at learning, perhaps this is the true secret to longevity.

There is no reason for the sages and saints to be unhappy. Confucius said: "Happiness lies within it." Yan Hui said: "Unchanging in its joy." Mencius regarded "not feeling ashamed or disgraced" as joy. The Analects begins with "happiness." The Doctrine of the Mean says "No one is not satisfied with themselves." The Neo-Confucianism of Cheng-Zhu seeks the joy of Confucius and Yan Hui, this is the intention behind it. The joy of the sages and saints, I dare not hope for, but just secretly emulate Bai Fu's kind of happiness, where "the old man at home, with white beard fluttering, wife and children are joyfully harmonious, roosters crow and dogs bark freely and leisurely."

Regardless of winter or summer, one should get up at sunrise, which is more suitable in summer. The qi of heaven and earth at sunrise is most refreshing for the spirit, and it is a pity to miss it. Living in the mountain temple, I always get up at sunrise in the summer, breathing in the fragrant smell of water and grass. The lotus buds are yet to bloom, the green bamboo glistens with dewdrops, it can be said to be the most enjoyable time. Summer days are long, a short nap during midday, with curtains drawn and incense lit, relaxing with a peach wood fan, sleeping until refreshed, feeling clear and refreshed. It's truly no different from the immortals in the sky.

Joy is suffering, suffering is joy. Some deficiencies, how do we know they are not blessings? When everything goes well in the family, and everything is satisfying to oneself, this bustling scene is actually a sign of desolation. Sages cannot avoid misfortune, immortals cannot avoid calamity, but it is precisely misfortune that forges sages, and calamities that refine immortals.

Wu Niu sees the moon and gasps for breath, the geese follow the sun and migrate south, constituting a busy world; bees gather flower scents, flies chase foul odors, all living lives of toil and labor. A life of toil and turmoil, all for the sake of fame and gain. Bound day and night, entangled in hot and cold, life and death are close at hand, all misled by the words fame and gain. Taking fame as charcoal to burn the soul, the soul's sweet spring will dry up; taking profit as venomous insects to sting the soul, the soul's spirit will be harmed. If you want a stable mind, to avoid illness, you must thoroughly rid yourself of fame and gain.

I read Tao Yuanming's "Idle Thoughts" and admired his devotion; I read "Returning Home Farewell" and admired his forgetfulness; I read "Mr. Five Willows' Biography" and admired his neither being sentimental nor unsentimental, devoted yet forgetful, truly incomprehensible. My friend Xia Dan'an admires Tao Yuanming the most, he reads without seeking deep understanding yet comprehends effortlessly, drinks without aiming to get drunk yet becomes intoxicated. And he said to me, "Why must poetry be in pentasyllabic form, why must officials hold high positions, why must one have five sons, why must there be five willow trees in the courtyard?" Truly, it can be said to be unrestrained and elegant! I dreamt of a couplet: "Five hundred years exiled in the mundane world, slightly turned into a game; Three thousand miles breaking through the vast sea, then it's freedom." Upon awakening, I told it to Zhuotang, who thought it was worth praising for its elegance, yet who can truly understand its profound meaning?

Master Liang from Zhending often tells people: Every evening at home, one must find something delightful and amusing, have hearty conversations with guests, stroke one's beard and laugh heartily, to dispel the gloominess accumulated throughout the day. This is truly grasping the essence of nurturing life.

Once, at a centenarian's birthday celebration in the countryside, I asked him about the secret to longevity. The old man said, "I am a countryman, I don't know anything about methods of nurturing life, but throughout my life, I only knew how to enjoy, never knew sorrow or trouble." Can this be achieved by people in the world of fame and fortune?

In ancient times, Wang Xizhi said, "I particularly enjoy planting fruit trees, there is a special joy in it. The trees I plant, when a flower blooms and a fruit grows, I particularly enjoy admiring them, and they taste even sweeter when eaten." Wang Youjun can truly find pleasure in it.

Lu You dreamt of the place where immortals reside, and wrote these poetic lines: "Beneath the long corridor, overlooking the blue lotus pond; The small pavilion faces the green rooster peak." Deeming it an extremely wonderful scenery. In the hermitage where I reside, such beautiful scenery stands out particularly, almost surpassing Lu Fangweng.

When I was in Ryukyu in the past, during the day I would stroll by the spacious pools, verdant mountain streams, tall pines and cypresses, and lush bamboo groves; at night I would light a lamp and read poems by Bai Juyi and Lu You. Lighting incense, brewing fragrant tea, inviting two gentlemen (referring to Bai Juyi and Lu You) to sit down, exchanging smiles with them, as if I had seen their indifferent and broad-minded hearts, almost wanting to abandon all things and follow them on a distant journey. This is also a method conducive to physical and mental pleasure.

After the age of forty-five, I began to focus on the method of tranquilizing the mind and nurturing the nature. The heart is the land of square inches, empty and clear, bright and awake, never allowing in any emotions of joy, anger, sorrow, or happiness, nor any worries or fears. It's like building a city, tightly closing the city gates, always strictly guarding against those few things from entering. Lately, I've noticed that they intrude less and less, and as the master resides in the city, there is peace and comfort.

The way to nurture oneself is to be vigilant against greed, cautious in diet, beware of anger, be alert to cold and heat, guard against delusions, and pay attention to fatigue. If any one of these is in the heart, it is enough to lead to illness, how can one not be cautious at all times! Master Zhang Ying (style name Dunfu) once said, "Ancient people understood the principles of nurturing life from reading the 'Selections of Literature,' relying on two sentences, namely: 'Stones hold jade and mountains shine; Water contains pearls and rivers charm.' " This is truly a profound statement. I have seen dewdrops on the stems of orchids and peonies, and if these dewdrops are eaten by ants, the flowers wither. I have also seen bamboo shoots just emerging, and every morning there are dewdrops at their tips. When the sun comes out, the dewdrops retract back to the base, and in the evening they climb up the tip of the shoot again. Elder Tianxian (Qian Chengzhi) wrote a poem: "In the evening, I see dewdrops on the tips of branches," describing this scene. If you enter the bamboo grove at dawn and see no dewdrops on the bamboo shoots, then they cannot grow into bamboo, you can dig them out and eat them as vegetables. There are also dewdrops on rice grains, appearing at night and retracting in the morning, all of a person's vitality is contained within them. Therefore, these two sentences from the "Selections of Literature" must be constantly observed to understand the essence of nurturing life, it's not about quantity.

My living space can only accommodate me stretching out my legs, in winter, the warm room is filled with various potted flowers, in summer, the window with curtains facing the tall ancient locust tree. What I enjoy between heaven and earth are just these things. However, stepping back, I have already received a lot from heaven, therefore, I am calm and peaceful, without envy or resentment. This is the joy of my old age.

    Master Pu said, "The human heart is particularly agile, one must not overwork, nor live too comfortably, only reading can nourish the mind." Those who are idle all day without reading, then no matter whether they are rising or falling, their body and mind have no place to rest, their eyes and ears have no place to rest, they are bound to be restless, give rise to many angers and complaints, and be unhappy in adversity or prosperity. The ancients once said, "Clean the house, light incense, and the blessings are already complete. Those blessed people accompany this with reading; while those without blessings will give rise to improper thoughts." This statement is extremely profound. Moreover, from ancient times to the present, for those who do not read, it seems that only their own experiences are painful, and thus extremely difficult to endure. But they do not know that the unpleasant things experienced by the ancients are a hundred times more unfortunate than their own experiences, they just did not carefully experience them! Like Su Dongpo, after his father Mr. Su Xun passed away, he was mourning heavily. Just as his essays were starting to gain attention, he was falsely accused and exiled, impoverished and destitute, wandering between Chaozhou and Huizhou, even wading across rivers barefoot, living beside cowsheds, what kind of scene is that? Or like Bai Juyi who had no offspring, or Lu You enduring hunger and hardship, these are all recorded in books. They are all famous figures for thousands of years, yet their experiences are like this. If one can truly look at life with equanimity, the unpleasant things in the world can melt away like ice. If one does not read, one will only see their own suffering as the most painful, and the endless resentment and anger will burn them, leaving them restless. Why do they have to suffer like this? Therefore, reading is the foremost task in nourishing one's old age.

    In Suzhou, there is Mr. Shi Zhuotang's old residence in the southern part of the city. The courtyard has the "Five Willows Garden," which exudes the charm of mountains, waters, springs, and rocks. Although it is within the city, it has the landscape of the outskirts, truly a good place for self-cultivation. Here, there are sounds like celestial music, rising and falling, echoing in my ears. The intermittent sounds emitted when birds sing in the woods; the rustling sounds when the breeze stirs the leaves; the murmuring sounds when the clear stream flows gently. I lie calmly on the verdant and lovely grass, gazing at the azure and clear sky, truly a marvelous painting! Comparing this place to the Humble Administrator's Garden, one is bustling while the other serene, truly surpassing the Humble Administrator's Garden.

We, as individuals, should seek ways to find happiness amidst unhappiness. Firstly, we must understand the causes of happiness and unhappiness, which of course are related to our environment, but the main reasons stem from within ourselves. Two people, facing the same circumstances, one can overcome adversity while the other is overcome by it. Those who can overcome adversity will feel comparatively happier when observing those who are conquered by it. Therefore, there's no need to envy others' fortunes or resent one's own misfortunes. This would only worsen the situation and ruin everything in life. Regardless of the circumstances, one should not be melancholic; instead, one should cultivate hope and happiness from within melancholy. I happened to discuss this insight with Shi Zhuotang, and he also agreed with it.

The family is like the declining autumn, the body is like the setting sun of dusk, emotions are like vanishing smoke, talents are like fleeting lightning. Thus, I am compelled to revel in paintings, indulge in poetry, wield my brush and ink freely, to express the joy in my heart. Just like how the grass leisurely admires its own flowers, and the birds, helpless, boast about their own voices. In early spring of February, when the clouds begin to clear, the mountains become bright, the birds become lively, and the plum blossoms bloom, that's when my poems and paintings come to life. Delighting in the plum blossoms, inspiring the birds, standing opposite the mountains, welcoming the clouds day and night, although my paintings are clumsy, I consider them skillful, and although my poems are written with hardship, I consider them sweet. The four walls have collapsed, a water gourd has broken, but nothing can harm this joyful disposition.

Master Pu drafted a couplet for me, intending to hang it in the cottage: "Riches and poverty are never satisfactory, contentment is true satisfaction; Mountains, waters, flowers, and bamboos have no permanent owners, leisure is being the true owner." Though the language is simple, it contains profound truths. There are countless beautiful mountains, waters, famous flowers, and bamboo, but perhaps those who pursue wealth and honor are driven by fame and fortune, and those who are poor are oppressed by hunger and cold, rarely able to appreciate these wonderful things. Being content and having leisure is true happiness, and it's also the best way to maintain one's life.

When the mind is not at rest, it's because various worries are affecting it, various thoughts are disturbing it. Just like the wind blowing over the water surface, causing ripples, this is not conducive to nurturing life. Generally speaking, those who practice sitting meditation cannot completely abandon their wild thoughts at first. At this time, one should focus on a single thought, gradually reaching a state of no thought, just like the water surface without a single ripple. After entering this state, one will feel infinite tranquility and be willing to share it with others.

Master Wang Yangming said, "As long as one's conscience is clear, even if one is taking the imperial exams, there's no need to exert oneself. For example, when studying, if one realizes that the idea of rote memorization is wrong, one should overcome it immediately; if one realizes that the idea of opportunism is wrong, one should overcome it immediately; if one realizes that the desire to boast is wrong, one should overcome it immediately. If one can do this, then one is simply engaging in dialogue with sages all day long, the heart is in accordance with the principles of nature, no matter how many books one reads, it's just nurturing this heart, where's the exhaustion?" I excerpted this passage as a rule for studying.

During Tang Wenzheng's (Tang Bin) tenure as the governor of Jiangsu, his daily food was only leeks. When his son occasionally bought a chicken, Tang Bin found out and rebuked him, saying, "Where is there a person who does not chew vegetable roots yet can achieve great things!" He then immediately returned the chicken. Why do those who eat meat all wish to have all the fat and oil to satisfy their appetites, thinking that it is what they deserve? But they don't know that sweet, crisp, and greasy foods are precisely the poison that corrodes the stomach. Generally, the cause of illness is definitely due to lack of moderation in diet. Frugality can cultivate integrity, and simplicity can reduce the expansion of desires. The rationale for contentment lies here, and the method for preventing disease also lies here. I like to eat garlic and have always avoided meat from butchers, always emphasizing frugality in food. Since Yunniang passed away, the plum blossom box has not been used again. I probably won't be rebuked by Tang Wenzheng, will I?

Zhang Liang, Duke of Ye Li Mi, secluded themselves in the ethereal place of white clouds; Liu Ling, Ruan Ji, Tao Yuanming, and Li Bai seclude themselves in intoxication; Sima Xiangru secluded himself in the gentle land of love; Mr. Chen Xiyi secluded himself in the dreamland of deep sleep, they all have a place to escape to. I believe that the land of white clouds is close to being ethereal, the land of intoxication and gentleness may not be conducive to curing diseases and prolonging life, but the land of sleep is the best. Stop all wild thoughts and wild words, and you can create a realm of ease. Quietly fall asleep and enter the dreamland, and soon you will reach a sweet and comfortable state. I often savor the taste of dreams after waking up, but I don't imitate the scholar on the Han Dan Road, borrowing a traveling immortal pillow from a Taoist to dream of wealth and honor.

There is no more important way to nurture life than sleep and diet. Even if the vegetable roots are rough, as long as they are eaten sweetly, they are better than precious delicacies. Sleep is also not about quantity, as long as it is truly refreshing and sweet, even if only for a moment, it is enough to nourish life. Lu You often delights in wonderful sleep, but there is also an art to sleeping. Master Sun said, "If you can calm the activity of the mind, naturally you can close your eyes." Cai Xishan said, "First sleep the mind, then sleep the eyes." This is indeed a wonderful method that others have not discovered. A Zen master told me that to make the mind calm and tranquil, there are three methods of sleep: the dragon's sleep, bending the knees when sleeping; the ape's sleep, hugging the knees when sleeping; the turtle and crane sleep, knees against knees when sleeping. When I was young, I saw my father take a short nap after lunch, and after turning on the lamp, he handled matters with a refreshed spirit. I have recently followed my father's practice, taking a nap on a bamboo bed after lunch, and sure enough, I feel refreshed in the evening. I increasingly believe in everything my father did, all of which can be imitated.

I may not be a monk, but I have the realm of a monk. Since Yun's death, I have become tired of all the worldly pleasures; I have felt compassion for all the worldly affairs. But time cannot be turned back, how can one not feel regret? In recent years, I have often discussed the "birthlessness" with the old monk. I have gradually begun to appreciate the joy of life. Kneeling and bowing to the Buddha, I rarely repent of my past sins, I offer poetry to the Buddha, and paintings as food for monks. Painting should have a calm temperament, poetry should have a lofty character. Even in painting and poetry, one must understand the Zen principles to reach a transcendent realm.

ABOUT THE AUTHOR

Shen Fu (1763-?) was a Chinese writer known for his work "The Six Records of a Floating Life." Born in 1763, Shen Fu lived during the Qing Dynasty. His masterpiece, "The Six Records of a Floating Life," showcases his keen observations of daily life and intricate portrayal of human emotions. Through delicate prose, Shen Fu captured the essence of personal experiences, offering readers profound insights into love, loss, and the transient nature of existence. Despite facing obscurity during his lifetime, Shen Fu's literary legacy has endured, cementing his reputation as one of China's most esteemed authors of the Qing era.

Printed in Great Britain
by Amazon